ROSWELL
HIGH

THE DARK ONE

by

MELINDA METZ

POCKET
BOOKS

An imprint of Simon & Schuster UK Ltd. A Viacom Company Africa House, 64-78 Kingsway, London WC2B 6AH

Produced by 17th Street Productions, Inc., 33 West 17th Street, New York, NY 10011

Copyright © 1998 by POCKET BOOKS A division of Simon & Schuster

A CIP catalogue record for this book is available from the British Library

ISBN 07434 08918

1 3 5 7 9 10 8 6 4 2

Printed by Omnia Books Ltd, Glasgow
First published in USA in 1998 by Archway Paperbacks.

ONE

"All of you, backs against the wall," Kyle Valenti ordered, his voice harsh. "Now!"

Michael Guerin obeyed, pulling Kevin DeLuca over to the bedroom wall along with him. He didn't know what that silver disk in Kyle's hand was, but Michael had seen its power. One blast from it had thrown him across the room and made the Stone of Midnight—the most powerful energy source on Michael's home planet—go dark and useless.

He positioned Kevin and himself between his brother, Trevor, and his best friend, Max Evans. He still felt the need to keep the two of them separated, even though Michael figured Max and Trevor were through trying to kill each other. For now at least, they had a common enemy.

Michael tightened his grip on Kevin's shoulder when he realized the kid was trembling. "Don't worry," he said softly. "We can take this guy."

Which was so true—usually. Usually Michael could take down Kyle without even using his powers. But with that weapon in Kyle's possession, who knew what Kyle was capable of?

"I said *all* of you." Kyle pulled Maria DeLuca out of the hallway behind him and shoved her into the bedroom. She raced over to Michael and squeezed in between him and Kevin, grabbing their hands.

"Kevin, I'm so sorry. This is all my fault," she said as Alex Manes, Liz Ortecho, Isabel Evans, and Adam rushed over and joined the line across the bedroom wall. "Are you okay? Did he hurt you?"

Michael hated hearing the fear in Maria's voice. Maria shouldn't have to feel afraid with him around. It was just . . . wrong.

"I'm okay," Maria's little brother answered.

Michael squeezed Maria's hand. "Kevin's fine," he promised her.

"Yeah," Kevin agreed weakly. "Fine."

"See? He can handle himself," Michael added, smiling at the little guy. Kevin was ten years old, and even if his words were brave, he was totally freaked. Michael figured the kid needed as much macho pride as he could muster to deal with this nightmare.

"There was an easy way to do this, and there was a hard way," Kyle announced. He strode from one end of the line to the other, looking each of them in the eye. "You chose the hard way. Fine."

Michael decided that Kyle was using a little macho pride to stay calm, too. There was no way Kyle could really be so in control, not after what he'd seen. Max and Trevor had been using their powers on each other with a vengeance. Kyle had to know he'd witnessed something a lot stranger than WWF Smackdown.

"But now you're going to tell me everything you know about my father," Kyle continued.

"Why should we tell you anything? After you decided to kidnap a little boy to—," Maria began, her voice edged with hysteria.

"Oh, shut up already!" Kyle barked.

Michael squeezed Maria's hand harder. She pulled in a deep, shuddering breath, glaring at Kyle.

"I ask the questions. You answer. That's how this is going to work," Kyle said.

He's doing his father, Michael realized. He's so wigged out that he's pretending to be big, bad Sheriff Valenti to get himself through this.

"Do you know who your father really worked for?" Max asked suddenly.

Kyle wheeled around and reached Max with three long strides. He pulled back his fist and slammed it into Max's stomach. "I said *I* ask the questions."

Michael could feel everyone in the room tense up as Max almost doubled over. He shot a warning glance at Isabel, and she gave him a reluctant nod. Michael knew it was taking all she had not to hurl herself at Kyle, make the connection, and squeeze one of the arteries in his brain until it popped. Which sounded like a good idea to Michael. He would have done it himself if it wasn't for the disk.

What *was* that thing?

It had to be a Project Clean Slate weapon, which

meant that it was designed for use on alien life-forms. Michael couldn't risk going after Kyle as long as he was holding it.

"Anybody else have a question?" Kyle demanded. "Or am I finally—"

Kevin let out a high shriek. It went on and on, shrill as an ambulance siren, and it made all the little hairs on the back of Michael's neck stand on end.

"Shut him up," Kyle ordered.

Maria pulled Kevin closer to her, but Kevin kept screaming, his eyes locked on the closet.

No, not the closet. All the saliva in Michael's throat dried up. Kevin's gaze was fixed on the network of veins that had begun to materialize in *front* of the closet.

"We've got company," Michael announced. He jerked his chin toward the veins. The heart was already forming, already *beating,* and the other organs appeared almost instantaneously—liver, pancreas, stomach, intestines, lungs.

"Dingdong. DuPris calling," Michael heard Alex mutter.

"What the hell is that?" Kyle bleated as muscle and bone began snaking between the organs. He backed up a step and stumbled, and the silver disk fell from his hand.

Michael didn't miss a beat. He hit the floor and snatched up the disk. Kyle didn't even notice. He was transfixed by the body forming in front of him. It was

4

complete now except for the empty eye sockets.

"I'm thinking we need a plan," Alex said. "I'm thinking it should involve running."

Too late. The bright green eyes of Elsevan DuPris materialized, and he pinned them with his gaze.

"Well, hello there, sweet children. I've missed you somethin' awful," he drawled, winking at them. "I thought you might be feeling nostalgic for the accent," he added, now without a trace of the southern twang he'd used for so long, parading around Roswell as the eccentric owner of the *Astral Projector* newspaper.

But he wasn't a reporter. He wasn't even human. He was, in fact, the being who had murdered Michael, Max, Isabel, and Adam's parents over fifty years before by causing their spaceship to crash into the desert in what became known as the Roswell Incident.

DuPris reached into his pocket and pulled out the Stone of Midnight he'd stolen from them. Unlike the one in Trevor's hand, DuPris's Stone gleamed with a green-purple light, pulsing with power.

Michael fingered the silver disk. If he could figure out how it worked, it could drain the power of the Stone, and without the Stone's power they might have at least a snowball's chance in hell of taking DuPris down. But if Michael made a mistake, the disk might also kill them all.

He was still debating whether to risk it when

Trevor stepped away from the wall and moved toward DuPris.

"Trevor! Stay back!" Michael ordered his brother. Trevor didn't even glance at him.

"You're the one," Trevor said, his eyes flicking from DuPris's face to the Stone of Midnight in his hand. "I came to this planet to deliver this to you." He held out the lifeless Stone. "But that one destroyed it before I had the chance." Trevor jerked his chin toward Kyle.

Michael's mouth dropped open as DuPris took the Stone, his green eyes glistening with eagerness. "It's not destroyed. It will regenerate its power."

"I want to be allowed to work with you," Trevor told DuPris. "I'm willing to give my life to see the collective consciousness shattered."

This was insane. Trevor was offering to *help* their enemy? Michael lurched away from the wall, pulling free of Maria. He strode to Trevor, grabbed him by the back of the shirt, and spun him away from DuPris. "You don't know what he is," Michael said urgently. "He killed our parents. He—"

"He is the only hope for the beings of our planet," Trevor interrupted, his gray eyes feverish. "Without him they will all be sucked into the consciousness. That's worse than death."

Michael fought for something to say—something to convince Trevor that he had DuPris all wrong, but he didn't have a chance.

"Oh, look at the time," DuPris exclaimed sarcastically. "We really must be going." He grabbed Trevor by the wrist, and their bodies began to disappear.

"No!" Michael yelled. "Trevor, you can't—"

He tried to make a grab for his brother, but nothing was left of Trevor except his eyes. His gray eyes, almost the exact color of Michael's. An instant later they vanished, too.

"No!" The scream felt like it ripped pieces of Michael's flesh from inside his body on the way out. His brother had joined up with DuPris. His *brother.*

"You want to know what happened to your father, Kyle?" Isabel asked, in full-on ice princess mode. "That *thing* killed him."

"He's dead? My dad's dead?" Kyle asked, his voice flat. He was still staring at the spot where DuPris and Trevor had been.

"I'm sorry," Liz told him.

Kyle didn't answer.

Michael couldn't help feeling for the guy. He remembered how crushed he'd been when he knew with absolute certainty that his parents were dead. It was like his body had frozen from the inside out, his heart almost too cold to continue beating.

Max walked up to Kyle, guided him over to the bed, and forced him to sit down. Then he sat beside him, glancing warily at his friends.

"I don't know how much you know, so I'll start at the beginning," Max said, his voice low and soothing, the way it would be if he were talking to a hurt animal. "Your father was with an organization called Project Clean Slate. Its mission was to hunt down . . . aliens, for experimentation and possibly extermination. DuPris is an alien. He went after your father and killed him. Destroyed the whole Project Clean Slate compound, too."

"I was the one who—," Adam began, sounding young and scared.

"Adam was there," Michael cut him off. "He was the one who saw what happened to your father." There was no reason for Kyle to know that DuPris used Adam's body to commit the murder. And if he had to pound Adam's pointy little head into the floor, someday Michael was going to get Adam to accept that.

"Aliens," Kyle repeated. "You expect me to believe that?"

But Kyle clearly did believe it. What choice did he have, after what he'd just seen? Michael wondered how long it would take him to figure out—

Kyle suddenly stood up, practically springing from the bed. "Then you are, too, right?" Kyle asked Max.

Max glanced from Michael to Isabel. Michael shrugged. It's not like Max really had a choice here. Yeah, he could try and feed Kyle some bull, but Kyle had seen too much.

"Yeah," Max answered. "I am."

"Get out of here," Kyle ordered. "I want all of you gone. I don't need you to—"

"To what? Get revenge?" Alex demanded. "Grow a brain, Kyle. With that Stone, even without it, DuPris could turn you into a pile of dust in a second, just like—"

Alex stopped before he said "your dad."

"Out!" Kyle screamed, his voice breaking.

This was one time when Michael was happy to take orders from Kyle Valenti. He took Maria's hand and headed for the door, but Kyle grabbed his arm as he passed, jerking him to a stop. "I'll take the device," he commanded. His voice was solid again, even though his eyes were petrified.

"No, I don't think you will," Michael answered.

"Give it to me, or I tell everyone—*everyone*— exactly what I saw here today," Kyle shot back. Michael didn't doubt that Kyle was telling the truth. The guy had nothing to lose, and that made him dangerous. Reluctantly Michael handed him the silver disk.

"With this thing I can turn off the Stone or whatever, right?" Kyle asked.

"Don't even think about it, Kyle," Michael warned. But he knew it was all Kyle was going to be able to think about. Michael understood about obsession.

"I think I'm going to go to bed," Kevin said, the second Maria and Michael got him home.

Maria couldn't remember a time that her little brother had volunteered to go to bed. "Why can't I stay up as late as Maria?" had been his constant question since he was old enough to talk. The fact that she was six years older than he was had never been accepted as a reasonable answer.

"Yeah. I'm sure you're tired. But Kev—" Maria glanced at Michael. "You know you can't talk about anything that happened, right?"

Kevin actually managed to grin at her. "You'd be in big trouble if Mom found out you let me get kidnapped," he said. Then the smile kind of slid off his face.

It wasn't the kidnapping part that bothered him. In some weird way, Kevin probably thought of that as an adventure, especially because the guy who kidnapped him wasn't much older than Maria. But the other stuff . . . Maria remembered how terrified she was when she had discovered the truth about Max, Michael, and Isabel. Suddenly she had no idea what to say.

"Here's the deal, Kevin," Michael said, surprising Maria by taking the initiative. "There are people out there who might want to hurt Max if they knew that he was . . . different. If you tell anybody what happened, they'd probably end up telling someone else—even if they promised they wouldn't."

He shot a look at Maria, and she knew he was remembering how Liz had broken her promise to Max by telling Maria the truth. And how Maria had then told Alex.

"You get what I'm saying?" Michael asked Kevin. "Eventually the wrong people could find out, and they might come and take Max away. Max, and me, and Isabel, and Adam."

Maria was surprised that Michael had given Kevin so much information. But it made sense in a way, at least revealing that he and Max were the same. Kevin knew Michael a lot better than he knew Max. Michael was around a lot, and Maria had realized a while ago that Kevin liked having a guy around. Sometimes living with just Maria and their mom got a little too female intensive for him.

"Why are you here?" Kevin blurted out. "I mean, why don't you live on your own planet?"

"Our parents came to Earth to see if it was a place that would accept colonization. They decided humans weren't quite, uh, ready to deal," Michael explained. "They were about to go home and tell everyone that, but their ship crashed. Max, Isabel, Adam, and I were in these incubation pods, and the pods survived. We were inside for more than fifty years, growing. Then we broke free, and—"

Michael must have noticed Kevin's eyes glazing over because he wrapped it up fast. "And that's why we live here. We don't have any way of getting back home."

Kevin nodded. He backed out of the living room. "I'm going to go to sleep."

"You want me to come tuck you in?" Maria asked.

Kevin gave her his most disgusted look.

"Sorry," she said quickly. Kevin turned and jogged down the hall.

"You're not going to offer to tuck *me* in, are you?" Michael joked after they heard Kevin's door shut.

The image of Michael lying in a bed rushed into Maria's mind. She shoved it right back out as fast as she could. She and Michael were in friend mode. She didn't know how much he was still thinking of Cameron, the girl that had squished his heart between her fingers, but she did know that whether he was thinking about Cameron or not, he certainly wasn't thinking about Maria. At least not *that* way.

"How about some antistress tea?" Maria asked, not wanting to even go near Michael's tucking-in question.

"Not right now." Michael flopped down on the couch, and Maria happily joined him. Even if Michael didn't think about her *that* way, he was still better than any antistress tea ever brewed. Just being near him, feeling the warmth emanating from his body, made her feel like . . . like purring or something. Even tonight. After all that had happened.

"Are you okay?" Maria asked. She didn't know how he could be. First his brother and Max, who was at least as much his brother as his biological brother was, had tried to kill each other. Then Trevor had joined up with DuPris, who had tried to kill them all not so long ago and who *had* killed Michael's parents.

And Max's, and Isabel's, and Adam's. And Trevor's.

"Did you just ask if I'm okay?" Michael scrubbed his hands through his black hair, making it even more spiky. "Me guy," he said, pointing at himself. "You girl." He pointed at her. "So don't be asking if I'm okay. If anyone asks anyone if they're okay, I'll be the one asking." He looked at her, his gray eyes unreadable. "So, are you okay?"

He's gone into lockdown, Maria thought. He's taking whatever it is he's feeling and caging it up somewhere. He doesn't get that that never works.

"I'm basically okay," Maria answered. "But I'm not the one whose brother just—"

"Went over to the dark side?" Michael interrupted. He stood up. "I'm going to head out. I want to see how Adam's doing."

"Call him. Tell him to come over," Maria answered. She didn't want Michael to leave. He was hurting so badly, he was about to shatter. Whether he'd admit it or not.

"Nah," Michael answered. "I don't want him to have to drag his butt over here. Adam's got to be wrecked."

"Project much?" Maria asked.

Michael groaned. "Don't be going all psychobabble on me. If you have to do something, just give me one of your vials of oil to sniff. At least that will only take a second."

"I know how much it meant to you to find out

you had a brother," Maria said, not letting him off the hook. "I think you should talk about—"

"You want me to talk?" Michael exploded. "Fine. My inner child, freaking little Mikey or whatever, is peeing in his pants because big brother Trevor turned out to be a freaking psycho. Okay? Happy now? Or what? You want me to cry for you? You want me to—"

"I just wanted you to—" Maria shook her head. This was pointless. Maybe someday he'd decide to let her in. But clearly not now. "Forget it."

"Fine," Michael snapped. He turned and strode toward the door. Maria followed him. He fumbled with the lock, cursing under his breath, and she reached around him and slid the bolt back for him.

He jerked open the door. Then, out of nowhere, he turned and pulled her to him. He hugged her so tightly, her ribs ached, but she didn't pull away. She held him as hard as her arms could manage—held him until he pulled away and left without a word.

TWO

Isabel crawled into bed, even though it wasn't anywhere near time for her two hours of sleep. Her bones ached. She could feel them each distinctly, feel the places where they connected to each other.

"I feel four hundred years old," she muttered. She rolled over onto her side, trying to find a comfortable position. It didn't help. The blankets felt too heavy. The weight of them made her bones throb. She kicked them off, wincing at the sound of one knee cracking.

That better not happen at cheerleading practice, Isabel thought. She could just imagine what Stacey Scheinin would say if she heard Isabel's bones creaking like some old person's.

Isabel shifted onto her back. She could feel each vertebra, as if there were no flesh between the bones and the mattress. Her pillow chafed against the back of her skull, and suddenly it was like she could feel each individual thread of the pillowcase pricking her head. She felt like her skull was being pierced by thousands of needles.

What is happening to me? she thought wildly. She

15

sat up fast, and the bottom sheet ground against the back of her legs. She gasped in pain.

Max. Have to get Max.

Isabel gritted her teeth against the pain and flung herself out of bed. The coarse strands of the carpet felt like they were shredding her feet. She stared down, expecting to see blood coating the floor, but there was none.

On her tiptoes so as little of her skin touched the carpet as possible, Isabel ran to the door. Even the smooth metal of the doorknob felt rough to her, but she managed to turn it and fling open the door.

Somehow she reached the stairs without screaming. And then she was fine again. The wood of the stairs felt pleasant under her feet.

Relieved, Isabel rushed down to Max's room. "The weirdest thing just happened," she exclaimed as she burst in after a quick knock.

Max didn't answer. Of course not, she thought. Some girls probably had brothers who hid out in their rooms to read *Playboy*. Isabel had a brother who closed himself in his bedroom to connect to the collective consciousness. Not that he wasn't partially connected all the time now.

Isabel snapped her fingers in front of his face. He was in deep. It gave her the creeps just looking at him, mouth slack, eyes staring off at nothing. I should take a picture of him so he can see how gross he looks, she thought. Not that Max would care. Her saintly brother was above caring about anything like his appearance—except for using his power to get rid of his zits.

"Max, I need to talk to you." Isabel gave his shoulder a shove. He didn't even blink. That had never happened before. Usually physical contact could bring him out of it.

She considered getting a glass of water and throwing it in his face but decided against it. The bizarre I-can-feel-my-own-bones sensation was gone, and Max . . . Max just wasn't that fun to hang out with anymore. Part of his attention was always on the consciousness now.

Isabel ran her foot across Max's carpet, pressing down hard, testing. No pain. No problem.

"It was probably a nightmare," Isabel muttered. "I was in bed and everything." She made her way back out into the hall, not bothering to be quiet. The whole house could explode around Max and his heartbeat would stay slow and steady.

She wandered into the kitchen, reluctant to go back to bed even though she still felt exhausted. That nightmare might still be there, waiting for her. A tiny shiver raced through Isabel's body.

"Wonder if Mom or Dad made it to the store," she whispered. The two of them weren't home yet. It wasn't even eight o'clock, and this was an out-of-Roswell day. They wouldn't make it home from their second law office in Clovis for at least half an hour. Isabel wished they would walk through the door right that second. A night watching one of those Lifetime movies with her mom while her dad made bad jokes would be the perfect nightmare antidote.

They'll be home soon, she told herself. She pulled open the freezer door. Ice cubes. And two boxes of peas frozen together. Plus lots of that clumpy frost. Definitely time to defrost. Isabel opened the lower door, turned the coolness setting all the way off, and started unloading the food onto the kitchen table. A cleaning project was almost as good as some Mom-and-Dad time. Not as much fun, but a good way to keep her mind off . . .

That nightmare. It hadn't really felt like a nightmare. It had felt real.

Oh, like it would be a nightmare if it felt totally fake, she thought sarcastically. She pulled open the vegetable crisper and wrinkled her nose at the broccoli, which had partially turned to slime. This was what happened when you had two lawyer parents who wanted to save the world. They tended to forget about the vegetable crisper.

Isabel reached over and grabbed a garbage bag from the cabinet under the sink. Then, using two fingers, she picked up the what-was-once-broccoli. Her stomach heaved as its stench reached her nose. It was as if the odor took on a physical mass as she breathed it in, coating her nose, sliding down her throat . . . and then expanding. The thick, foul-tasting mold left too little room for air. Isabel wheezed, struggling to pull a breath through the pinholes that were her nostrils and her throat.

"Max! Help!" She didn't have enough breath to scream. She was going to suffocate right there in her own kitchen.

No! Isabel would not let that happen. She jammed one of her fingers down her throat. If she could just get a little of the mold out, she'd be able to get some oxygen in. Her throat convulsed with a gag reflex, but she hadn't even touched the mold.

Isabel stumbled to the sink. She turned on the cold water full blast. If she could drink some, maybe—

And her throat was clear. Her nose was clear. It was as if the mold had never been there. As if it had been a horrible . . .

Nightmare.

But she was awake. Wide awake. And she'd been awake the whole time. Slowly, carefully, on legs that felt too weak to carry her, Isabel crossed to the kitchen table and lowered herself into the closest chair.

This is what happened to Max when he began to enter his *akino*, she realized. Heightened physical sensation. Physical sensation—like touch, like smell.

Isabel lowered her head into her hands. Max would tell her not to worry. He'd tell her that connecting to the collective consciousness and sharing your life with all the beings of the home planet—living and dead—was awesome, that it made you appreciate all the little things in your life when you felt the beings experience them with you.

To Isabel it sounded like prison. Always being watched. No privacy. No choice about who you let into your life.

And Isabel would rather die than be in prison.

Liz sighed as Max rapped the top of the table at Flying Pepperoni.

"So since we're all here, I guess we should talk about what we're here to talk about," he said.

He looked around the booth, but his gaze skittered over Liz. She didn't think he'd really looked at her once since she broke up with him.

"What about Alex?" Isabel asked.

"He said he had plans," Maria answered.

"Plans more important than figuring out how to deal with a sociopath who now has two—count 'em, two—of the three Stones of Midnight?" Michael picked up the pepper shaker and shook some directly onto his tongue.

"We can fill him in later," Liz said. She didn't want to waste fifteen minutes debating the subject. Working together to find Kevin after he'd been kidnapped was one thing. But sitting this close to Max without a life-or-death situation as distraction was killing her. She was as far away from him as she could get, but in a booth that was still close.

It didn't help that Adam was looking at her as much as Max was *avoiding* looking at her. Liz had the feeling that Adam was hoping her breakup meant there were . . . possibilities between them. She flicked a glance at him and was unsurprised to find his green eyes on her.

Lucinda Baker strolled up to their table. "Okay? What?" she asked, tapping her order pad with her pen.

"Half everything. Quarter veggie special. Quarter meatball and pineapple," Max told her.

Lucinda rolled her eyes. "Hey, where's the cute one?" she asked.

"I'm right here," Michael bragged, leaning back in his seat.

"No, the *cute* one. Um, I always forget his name," Lucinda said. She frowned, concentrating. "Alex! So, where's Alex?"

"Alex? Alex Manes?" Liz asked.

She loved Alex. He was her best boy bud. But the reason that Lucinda didn't remember his name was that most of the girls at school had always been oblivious of just how great Alex was.

Maria leaned close. "The wormhole beauty treatment," she whispered in Liz's ear.

Liz nodded. DuPris had tricked them into sending Alex through a wormhole and back to the aliens' home planet in DuPris's place. When Alex had come back through another wormhole—followed by Trevor—he looked, not different exactly, but just *more*. Hair a richer red. Eyes a deeper green. Body

21

somehow thicker? Stronger? It was hard to pinpoint all the changes, but the overall effect clearly made an impression.

Liz realized Lucinda was still waiting for an answer. "Alex had plans," she said.

"Well, tell him I said hi, okay?" Lucinda licked her bottom lip, then headed off.

"She would eat our little Alex alive," Michael commented.

"I don't know about that," Isabel answered. She sounded a bit depressed by the thought. Liz wondered if she had regrets about breaking up with Alex.

Maybe she's just tired, Liz thought. Isabel had the look of someone who'd experienced a very bad night. Liz had seen that look on her own face often enough lately, after nights thinking about how the collective consciousness was pulling Max away from her and—

"So does anyone have any suggestions?" Max asked, again doing a check of every face at the table except Liz's.

Michael did another pepper shot. "I don't even know why we're here. Like I said, DuPris has two of the Stones. Plus a new sidekick, my *brother*. When he had one of the Stones and was the Lone Ranger, he almost killed us all. What could you possibly think we could do? Start a petition?"

Maria and Liz exchanged a look. Michael was never exactly Mr. Sunshine, but his tone was so bitter, it made Liz's stomach curl up. His brother's betrayal had clearly devastated him.

"Michael's right," Adam agreed. He was speaking to Max, but his eyes kept darting to Liz. "DuPris is too strong to fight. He could take over any one of us anytime."

Adam didn't sound bitter. He sounded resigned. Maybe that's what happened when you grew up the way Adam did, Liz thought. After spending most of his life being held prisoner by Sheriff Valenti in Project Clean Slate's underground compound, Adam probably just assumed that very bad things could happen at any moment.

"And he would only decide to take us over if he felt like using the subtle approach," Michael jumped in again. "Otherwise we could all just be pushin' up friggin' daisies before we can blink."

Adam looked a little confused. There were still a few gaps in his education on life in the real world.

"What Michael is trying to say, in his tactful manner, is that we'd be . . . dead," Maria explained.

"So are you saying we should just give up? Roll onto our backs?" Max demanded.

Isabel pulled a ragged napkin out of the metal napkin holder and adjusted the one beneath it so it was tightly tucked. "There's something I want to discuss before we talk about destroying DuPris," she announced.

"What could be more important?" Max snapped.

He shoved his hand through his blond hair. "You heard DuPris. He and Trevor are going to try to shatter the consciousness—"

"Exactly," Isabel interrupted. "I don't know about the rest of you. But I'm not sure shattering the consciousness is such a bad idea."

Thank you, Isabel, Liz thought. She'd been wanting to say the same thing, but she knew if she did, Max would just accuse her of hating the consciousness because it interfered with their kissing. He just didn't understand how much he'd changed. How when he was in the deep connection, he wasn't Max anymore.

"Good point," Michael said. "I for one don't want to walk around like a pod person." He turned to Max. "No offense."

"I'm not a pod person," Max protested, obviously frustrated. "I choose when to deepen the connection."

"*Sometimes* you choose," Liz corrected, unable to hold back. "Not always. Not lately. More and more often you . . . go off, whether you decide to or not."

Max looked like he was about to snap, but Michael cut him off.

"Like at Kyle's," Michael said. He picked up the pepper shaker and twirled it between his fingers, appearing fascinated by the movement. "Was it all you who tried to kill my brother? Or did you have *help*?"

"In case you've forgotten, your *brother* was trying

to kill *me*. Or doesn't that matter since I'm not a relation?" Max snatched the pepper shaker out of Michael's hand.

"All I'm saying is that it's not like you to set your phaser on kill, you know?" Michael said. "Usually you would go for something less extreme. Like containment."

"DuPris is evil," Maria cut in. She nibbled the end of one of her blond curls, something she did only under extreme stress. "Are you and Isabel saying we should just, like, send him a muffin basket and wish him the best on annihilating the consciousness?" she asked Michael.

"What I'm saying is that the scenario we have going is bugs and Raid. We're the bugs," Michael answered. "Whether we agree with what DuPris is trying to do or not—he's got all the power."

"There is the device that Kyle had," Liz reminded them, pulling her long, dark hair back from her face. "That could be an equalizer."

"Except Kyle's not going to let us have it," Isabel said, sounding the faintest bit relieved.

"Maybe we could duplicate the technology," Liz responded.

"Gee, Captain Wizard, you're right. Adam has a toaster. And I have a couple of forks. That's all we'd need," Michael volunteered with mock enthusiasm.

Liz ignored him. "I'm just saying that we don't have to just roll over if we don't want to."

For the first time since the breakup Max looked at Liz, really looked at her, full force, his blue eyes bright with emotion. "Are you saying you're on my side? You think what DuPris wants to do to the consciousness is a desecration?"

Liz noted the choice of the word *desecration* and the fervor with which Max spoke but didn't comment on it. "I didn't say that," she told him. "I agree with Maria—DuPris is evil." She hesitated. "But I also agree with Isabel and Michael. I don't like what the consciousness is doing to you. You're losing yourself, and because you are, you aren't even able to recognize that it's happening."

"You can't have it both ways, Liz," Max said.

She tried to remember if it was the first time he'd said her name since they broke up. "I think in this case I can," she answered slowly. "I think it's possible for the right thing to be done for the wrong reasons. Just because DuPris is evil does not mean that shattering the consciousness is evil, although I'm sure his methods for achieving it would be ruthless."

"The right thing for the wrong reasons," Max repeated.

Liz nodded. Or the wrong thing for the right reasons, she thought. Like breaking up with Max. It hurt so much, it had to be the wrong thing. But her reasons were right. She was sure of that. She had to break up with him because he wasn't the Max she had fallen in love with.

"I don't think this is going to work," Max said. He gestured around the table. "I don't think that there is any plan or course of action that we'll all be able to agree on. Because as far as the right thing for the wrong reason—I think that's bull."

"He's right. We're never going to agree." Maria sounded close to tears.

It used to be so much easier, Liz thought. She remembered the day they'd come up with the plan to fake an alien's death and throw Valenti off Max's trail. That magical day when they'd all connected for the first time in a swirl of color, sound, scent.

Their bond was so pure. So intense.

And now . . . there were stress cracks everywhere in their group. Between her and Max. Between Isabel and Michael and Max. Between Adam and Max, whether either of them would acknowledge it or not. Between her and Adam because Adam wanted more than Liz thought she could give him. Between Maria and Michael for the same reason—Maria wanted more. And Alex—the guy hadn't even bothered to show up.

"One disgusting pizza." Lucinda Baker stepped up and dropped the pie on the table, the tin pan clattering.

"I'm not really hungry," Isabel said.

"Neither am I," the rest of them said, almost in unison.

Liz wondered if it was the last thing they'd ever agree on.

THREE

Alex leaned against the railing of the mall's upper level and stared down at the fountain below. He was supposed to meet Stacey Scheinin there in fifteen minutes. Stacey Scheinin—as in head cheerleader, as in one of the most popular girls in school.

As in what could she possibly want with Alex Manes? Okay, he had gone out with Isabel Evans. And in his book—and in the books of plenty of guys at school—Isabel ranked higher than Stacey in terms of hotness and just general *it*-ness.

But Isabel never would have shown the slightest interest in him if he hadn't learned her secret. That had forced them together. It had given her a chance to see him as more than one of the horde of average guys who worshiped Princess Isabel from afar. She'd gotten to see he was someone she could count on. Someone—

Someone that, ultimately, she didn't want to be with. Surprisingly, the pain of that realization had almost faded away completely. Or maybe not so surprisingly. Maybe that's what happened when you got zapped away to another planet where a faction of the beings wanted you dead. Things just sort of fell into perspective.

Alex scanned the area around the fountain. There were no suspicious clumps of giggling girls or smirking guys waiting to mock him for falling for the biggest practical joke ever. Weird as it was, it seemed like Stacey had been totally sincere when she had invited him to meet her here. It wasn't some high-school-ritual-humiliation kind of thing.

Alex pushed himself away from the railing and wandered toward the food court. There was no way he would be waiting at the fountain like some anxious little puppy when Stacey showed. He'd get there when they agreed to meet, but not any earlier.

When he reached the first of the little food stands, Alex turned around. Okay, he didn't want to appear too eager, but that didn't mean he wanted to meet Stacey with questionable breath or the potential of some kind of mall food gunk stuck to his front teeth. He turned into the Gap instead. Nothing was safer than the Gap.

"Excuse me," a woman called, a tall, gorgeous woman who looked like she should be on a magazine cover and not in a dinky mall in Roswell. "I need a male opinion. Does this sweater look good on me?"

Alex knew she wasn't talking to him, but if she was, he'd have to say there wasn't a guy alive who wouldn't like her in that sweater—or anything else.

"Excuse me," the woman said again. Alex glanced

around to see what fool could possibly be ignoring her and realized *he* was the fool. She was actually talking to him.

"That sweater should be paying *you* to wear it," he told her, pulling out one of his older brothers' lines. And then she laughed. Actually laughed in a flirty way. Good God almighty, *she* was flirting with *him*. I've gone through another wormhole, he thought. I'm on a planet of inverse male attractiveness. First Stacey Scheinin asks me on a could-be date, and now this.

He glanced at his watch and saw that he had only a few minutes to make it to the fountain on time. "You should buy it. Really," he called to the woman.

"You're leaving?" she asked, giving him a sexy little pout.

"Sorry," he said as he headed out the door. Definitely a strange new world. That was the only place a woman could direct one of those little pouts in his direction.

Alex trotted down the stairs instead of taking the escalator, feeling light and buoyant. As long as he was visiting this wonderful planet, he was going to enjoy it.

"I've been waiting two whole minutes," Stacey called from her seat on the rim of the fountain, spotting him before he spotted her. She gave him a pout, too.

"Two whole minutes without me? Are you all right?" Alex teased, confidence soaring after he'd scored two real-life, sexy pouts in less than ten minutes.

"I will be once you get your butt over here," she answered playfully. Alex knew Isabel hated Stacey's high, breathy voice, but Alex thought it was kind of cute.

Alex walked over to her, not too fast, and when he reached her, Stacey wrapped her arm around his waist, surprising him. He didn't expect her to get even a little physical so fast. Actually he didn't expect her to get physical at all.

Not that he was complaining or anything. He looped his arm across her shoulders, which he thought was the best response to the waist wrap. The double waist wrap, where the guy slid his arm around the girl's waist, made walking difficult. And the hand-in-the-girl's-back-pocket wasn't a move for amateurs. Unfortunately, Alex felt like he still fit in that category.

"Aren't those the most adorable little strappy pumps?" Stacey cried, towing Alex toward A Walk on the Moon, the mall's shoe store. And they were off. Doing the promenade. Window shopping, or at least pretending to, but mainly walking the lower loop of stores, checking out who was with whom and being checked out in return.

Alex caught an envious look from Craig Cachopo, who was selling shoes since he'd quit his UFOnics job. He gave Craig a cool little yeah-I-know-we-go-to-the-same-school nod, and then Stacey was propelling him to the next store.

"Oh, that's tacky," she announced, shaking her head at a denim dress with a big sequined sunflower over the pocket. There was no one from school in the vicinity of that store, and Stacey kept them moving along. Alex just went with the flow, picking up another envious look as Stacey came to a stop in front of the jewelry store. "Aren't those the most adorable little earrings you've ever seen?" she exclaimed.

Alex murmured something agreeable. He spotted Steve Lydick, center of the basketball team, coming at them from the opposite direction. Alex pretended to study the jewelry display with Stacey, but he kept track of Steve from the corner of his eye. He knew the exact second that Steve saw him with Stacey— because a second after *that* Steve dropped his ice-cream cone on one of his size-thirteen sneakers.

Stacey caught the spill and giggled. "Hope we don't see you doing anything like that on the court," she called, hustling Alex over to a combination Indian artifacts–alien souvenir shop. She pointed to an inflatable green alien wearing a rhinestone tiara.

"How awful is that?" she said snidely. "Who would buy that thing?"

"Royalty should never be mocked that way," Alex said solemnly. "What would Princess Diana have said?"

"Exactly," Stacey said, smiling up at him.

Alex's eyes wanted to roll very badly, but he wouldn't let them. Yeah, Stacey was a fluffhead, but he was finding it amusing to spend an afternoon as

33

part of the elite. When he and Isabel had made one of their few public appearances, people had always been whispering behind their backs, speculating on what she could possibly see in him.

But that wasn't happening with Stacey. Alex even caught a few girls shooting them glances that seemed to be asking what *he* saw in *her*. But no. That wasn't possible. He was probably just heady from Stacey's perfume.

After one full mall circuit and many "isn't that adorable" and "oh, that's tacky"s, Alex was thinking maybe the whole popularity thing was a huge sham. Were all popular people as bored as he was right now? Was Stacey actually enjoying this?

"Okay, there's still one place we haven't gone yet," Stacey said coyly. She maneuvered him into a tiny alcove with a drinking fountain and one bench. In all the years he'd been coming to the mall, Alex had never even seen it before.

"Is there something adorable or tacky back here?" he joked.

A tiny wrinkle appeared between Stacey's eyebrows. "You mean you don't want to?" she asked.

And then he got it. He'd just been initiated into one of the mall make-out areas. He sat on the bench and pulled Stacey down next to him. That's all the invitation she needed. A moment later her soft, bubble-gum-lip-gloss-flavored mouth was busy kissing him.

I don't even like this girl, Alex thought. Liz would have a fit if she could see me. She'd say I'm shallow and superficial and—

Stacey nipped his earlobe as if she could sense that his mind was wandering. Alex responded by concentrating on kissing the side of her neck until she was squirming with delight.

Forget Liz, he thought. This is just for fun. And I was held prisoner on a hostile planet. If anyone deserves some just-fun time, it's Alex Manes.

"This is an exact replica of the Partridges' living room," Elsevan DuPris told Trevor. "I'm assuming you have heard of *The Partridge Family*. 'Really came together when Mom sang along,'" he warbled.

"I've seen a couple of episodes. The materials about Earth provided by the Kindred were very detailed," Trevor answered. He shifted uncomfortably on the sofa. It didn't feel right to be sitting so close to the leader of the rebellion—the being Trevor had idolized for as long as he could remember.

"Ah, the Kindred," DuPris said. "How are those of the Kindred?"

"It is becoming more and more difficult for them to stay hidden from those who have joined the consciousness," Trevor explained, eager to prove his usefulness to DuPris. "But obtaining the second Stone of Midnight and knowing it is in your hands has given them more hope than they have felt in generations."

DuPris nodded. "The era of the consciousness is almost over. Someday historians will look back at it and see it for the barbaric creation it was. They will realize it reduced sentient beings to the state of hive insects without individual freedom or even the *desire* for individual freedom."

"I will do anything to help you shatter the consciousness," Trevor vowed. "I will make any sacrifice."

He had dreamed about having the chance to say those words to the rebel leader for so long, but a lance of pain ripped into him as he flashed on what he'd already lost. Michael was his brother, his only living relative. He'd welcomed Trevor into his home, into his life. And now—

DuPris reached out and grabbed Trevor by the wrist. Trevor felt a tingling sensation in his brain and then a searing burst of heat.

"Thinking about your brother. How sweet," DuPris said sarcastically. He let Trevor go, then combed his slicked-back hair with his fingers. "Don't you see that sentiment for family groupings is the same kind of thinking that brought about the creation of the consciousness? Every being must take responsibility for itself. It is the only way our planet will ever reach its full potential."

Trevor nodded, clamping down on the burst of anger he felt at DuPris for reaching in and snatching thoughts out of his head. He hoped there weren't any traces of the anger flickering in his aura. DuPris deserved complete loyalty. It was through him that the beings of the Kindred would gain their freedom.

"The first thing we have to do is reinvigorate the damaged Stone of Midnight." DuPris pulled a piece of velvet out of his pocket. He unwrapped it, revealing the lifeless Stone. "Every day you and I will connect and join powers, then send energy into the Stone. In several weeks it will be back to its full strength," he continued, placing the Stone on the table.

Again DuPris took Trevor's wrist. A few moments later the connection was made, and images from DuPris's mind invaded Trevor's.

An almond-shaped, pupil-less eye being cut from its socket by a clawed finger. A body consumed by fire, tentacles waving until they shriveled to dead strings. A mother and baby felled by a taser blast.

"No. No. Don't make me see it." Trevor's human body responded to his horror, his heart thrashing in his chest.

But the images kept coming. A hand reaching into a metal-studded abdomen as if it were as soft as clay and pulling free the secondary appendage. A young boy being forced to watch as his father was tortured.

Trevor tried to jerk his hand free, but DuPris tightened his grip, fingers brutal. "Little boy, did you actually think a revolution could be fought without blood?" DuPris asked, the question detonating in Trevor's head.

"I misjudged you," DuPris continued. "I thought

that you were ready to join the rebel force, to work side by side with me."

"I am," Trevor gasped, fighting against the nausea still sweeping through his body in response to what he'd seen. "I am," he said again, more forcefully. This was what he'd been waiting for his whole life. Nothing was more important than the shattering of the consciousness. Nothing.

"Then join your power with mine," DuPris instructed, loosening his grip slightly.

Trevor focused every molecule of his being on building a power ball with DuPris. Expanding it out, out, out until his body trembled with the strain.

DuPris gave the signal, and he and Trevor hurled their ball of power at the Stone. Trevor opened his eyes—he hadn't even realized he'd closed them—and looked down at the Stone. Some of its green-purple light had returned. Not much more than a flicker. But it was the most beautiful thing Trevor had ever seen.

"You did well." DuPris released Trevor and clapped him on the shoulder. "There are many who brag about being willing to sacrifice anything, then fall apart at the first real test."

Trevor kept his eyes on the Stone. "I want to ask you something," he told DuPris.

"So ask." DuPris sounded bored.

"Michael said you killed . . . our parents." Trevor forced himself to look directly into the rebel leader's eyes.

"I'm sure you know the history of the cause," DuPris answered. "I stole one of the Stones of Midnight and escaped with it by stowing away on a ship—your parents' ship. I planned to use Earth as my base until I acquired the other two Stones necessary to destroy the consciousness."

Faint threads of red appeared around DuPris, and Trevor realized for the first time that the rebel leader had managed to cloak his aura. Just those few streaks of anger were visible, and they quickly vanished.

"Your parents were the only two members of the rebellion on the ship, something that, of course, was kept secret from the others," DuPris continued. "When the others discovered my presence on the ship, they imprisoned me. They planned to return me to our planet for judgment by the consortium."

Tears sprang to Trevor's eyes. He had learned about the way the human body responded to emotion in the materials given to him by the Kindred, but he was still taken aback every time his feelings affected him physically. He blinked quickly, hoping DuPris hadn't noticed Trevor's wet eyes.

"So you caused the ship to crash," Trevor said, struggling to keep his voice steady.

"A necessary sacrifice. I had to keep the Stone in my possession," DuPris replied.

"A necessary sacrifice," Trevor replied. He understood the logic. The lives of a few beings could not be allowed to cripple the rebellion.

"Any more questions?" DuPris asked. "I want to get back to redecorating the master bedroom. I've chosen a Mr. and Mrs. Brady theme."

"No more questions," Trevor answered.

Within moments DuPris had teleported out of the room.

Trevor returned his gaze to the Stone, allowing its beauty to calm him. The power of the Stones will bring all on my planet freedom, he thought. *Freedom.*

He'd been taught from childhood that the rebellion demanded sacrifice and that it was a gift to be asked to give an offering.

"I have sacrificed all I have," he whispered. "I have given the rebellion everything. It is an honor." Trevor felt tears sting his eyes again. Frustrated with his body, he wiped them away with his sleeve.

FOUR

Michael walked through the front door of his house—or tried to. He didn't get very far because his dad blocked his way.

"You don't live here anymore," he told Michael. "We decided we don't want you. You're staying across the street now."

"Oh, okay," Michael said, trying to sound casual, as if his dad had just asked him to run to the store or something. "Can I get my stuff?"

"You don't have any stuff. We gave you everything you had, and we're keeping it," his father told him gruffly. He gave Michael a push, and he stumbled back out onto the front walk. Michael didn't wait around to be pushed twice. He turned and bolted, his heart pounding like crazy. He started toward the house directly across the street but froze when he saw a woman in the front yard. She was holding a shotgun, aiming it directly at his chest.

"We don't have any more room here," she announced.

"But my dad said—," Michael began.

The woman cocked the rifle. "Another step and

you'll be pushin' up friggin' daisies," she warned him.

Scared out of his mind, Michael took off down the street . . . and found himself in the doughnut shop, a plate of crullers loaded with hot sauce in front of him.

"Nice dream you were having," Trevor commented as he appeared in the seat across from Michael.

Michael spit out the bite of cruller he'd just taken. "Listen carefully. I don't ever want to see you again. If I do see you again, you are not going to be a happy guy."

"I want to explain—," Trevor began.

"Explain what?" Michael demanded. "Explain why you betrayed me? Why you fed me that line about coming here just to visit your long lost brother? Or explain about why you tried to kill Max? Or maybe why you've decided to become the lapdog of the guy who killed our parents?"

"Actually, all of that," Trevor answered, gazing intently at Michael. As always Michael felt startled by how alike his eyes and Trevor's were. "You're the only family I have left," Trevor continued. "And by the way, your good friend Max? He tried to kill me, too."

Michael pushed the plate of crullers aside and rested his elbows on the Formica table. "You want to explain?" he said. "Fine. Start with why you lied to me, and go from there."

"I was sent to Earth to take the Stone from Alex and give it to the rebel leader. You call him DuPris,"

Trevor began, all business. "I was chosen for the mission because as your brother—"

"You could infiltrate the group," Michael finished for him, his eyes flashing. "So you used me. What the hell? It's not like we knew each other or anything. We were just brothers." He hated the emotion he could hear coursing through his voice. He hated that Trevor actually had the power to . . .

To hurt him.

"You've got to understand about the consciousness. It's evil, Michael," Trevor explained. "Shattering it is more important than saving the feelings of any individual. Me. You."

"Our parents?" Michael demanded, feeling his face redden. "Did you ask your idol about them?"

"Yeah. I did," Trevor admitted. He hesitated, staring down at the pink tabletop as if it fascinated him.

"He didn't deny it, did he? And you're still working for the guy." Michael jerked to his feet. "That's all I need to hear." He started toward the door, but Trevor grabbed him by the elbow and hauled him back.

"No, it's not all you need to hear," he said harshly, his fingers pressing into Michael's flesh.

"Let go of my arm," Michael ordered.

"Not until you—"

Michael didn't let him finish. He pulled back his free arm, made a fist, and slammed it into Trevor's jaw. Trevor loosened his grip, and Michael started for the door again. This time one of the tables screeched across the room and barricaded the exit. "Oh, you want to play." Michael turned to face his brother. There was no need to worry about who had more powers in the dream plane. If Michael thought something, it would happen. At least once he realized he was dreaming, which, thanks to Trevor, Michael did.

In a flash a second table knocked Trevor to the ground and pinned him to the floor.

"Are you afraid of what you're going to hear? Is that it?" Trevor cried.

The table on top of him exploded into Formica shards, sharp as knives. Every one of them flew straight at Michael.

Michael didn't even flinch. He *thought* them right back at Trevor, who spun them around again. The shards hovered between them, shaking as Michael and Trevor both tried to control the weapons.

"If our parents hadn't died—," Trevor began, face tight with concentration.

"Been murdered," Michael corrected, keeping his attention focused on the shards.

"Then the Stone of Midnight that DuPris stole would have been returned to our planet," Trevor said in a rush. "The rebellion might have been squashed. All those in the Kindred might have been forced to join the consciousness."

"So it's okay to kill anyone who gets in the way of the rebellion?" Michael demanded, clenching his fists.

"Yes!" Trevor shouted.

"No!" Michael shouted back.

The shards fragmented and fell to the floor in a shower of powdery dust. Michael and Trevor locked eyes for a long moment. Then, without warning, Trevor disappeared.

I have to get out of here, Michael thought, his body practically shaking from all the effort and emotion he'd expended. The table slid away from the door at Michael's thought command.

"Wait. What am I doing?" he said. He concentrated a moment, and the shimmering, iridescent walls of his dream orb appeared. He stepped through and woke up.

The sheet under Michael's back was moist with sweat. This was not a problem because Michael had no intention of going back to sleep anytime soon. He glanced at the clock on the bedside table and found that it was three-thirty in the morning. He'd gotten most of his two hours of sleep.

Michael stood up and pulled on his jeans and a T-shirt. He hesitated a moment, then slid on his shoes, too. It seemed like a good time for one of his late night visits to Maria's room. She never minded him waking her up, and somehow he always ended up feeling a little better after spending time with her. Even if she drove him crazy with too many questions.

He headed out of the bedroom down the hall, glancing at Adam as he passed. Michael paused. Adam had probably gotten most of the sleep he needed, too, and he was always up for hanging out. Maybe he should just stay here and chill out. Teaching Adam some more about life in the real world would definitely take his mind off things. For a little while, anyway.

But the more he thought about it, Michael realized it wasn't Maria or Adam he wanted to be with right now. He needed to see Max. Things had gotten bad between them, and it was time for that to end.

"He's my real brother, anyway," Michael muttered. "Enough is enough."

Max rubbed his rubber Koosh ball up and down the side of his face. A cluster of the beings in the consciousness never seemed to tire of the sensation, and through them Max shared the deliciousness of the rubber strands bushing against his skin. Their pleasure was almost as intense for Max as anything he'd ever experienced on his own.

Reluctantly he dove away from the Koosh-loving beings and pushed himself deeper into the ocean of auras that made up the consciousness. He focused on an image of Ray Iburg and shot it out into the billions of entities. There was a faint ripple of response, not from Ray himself, but from beings who knew of Ray.

Max caught a current and surfed into another section of the consciousness. He wanted to call Ray from a different spot. Ray was the only adult survivor of the crash—at least the only one who wasn't evil incarnate. He'd taught Max so much before he'd died. If Max could just talk to him—or exchange images and emotions the way the beings in the consciousness did—maybe Ray would have some clue what he should be doing. Because everything in Max's life was falling apart, and there was no one Max could talk to about it. He was the only one on Earth who was connected to the consciousness, and he needed advice from the only other being who had been connected while living on Earth.

Plus he wouldn't mind one of Ray's Elvis impersonations. Something to make Max laugh would be nice. I could always go back to the Koosh crowd, he thought. But it was too easy to lose time in a cluster of auras like that one, too easy to get seduced by the pleasure of physical sensation, amplified as it was by the beings.

Max focused on an image of Ray in his spangled Elvis jumpsuit and sent it out. This time there wasn't even a flicker of recognition, although he caught some amusement and a little fear.

Another current swept past him. Max allowed himself to be drawn along with it and was sucked into a massive aggregation of ice-cold auras. These beings are terrified, he realized. Terrified that DuPris has two of the Stones. Terrified of . . . of dying.

Max tried to throw out a question, but the cold

had seeped too deeply into him. He'd been frozen to the point that he was incapable of throwing the necessary images to find out why the beings feared they were close to death.

Above him he felt a current passing. He tried to propel himself up to meet it. But the numbing coldness made it impossible.

"Max," a voice cried, so far away, Max couldn't make out who was speaking. "Max!" It came louder, and this time Max realized it was Michael calling to him.

The sound of Michael's voice jolted him free of the icy block of auras, and Max found himself speeding along in the current. He had started to break the connection to the consciousness—well, turn down the volume, at least—when a group of beings demanded to know about the odor Max was smelling.

Max concentrated, then sent back the answer— lemon-scented furniture polish. Then they asked him what a lemon was. Max focused on imagining a lemon tree with as much detail as he could.

"Max!" he heard Michael call, soft as a whisper.

Be there in one second, he thought. He threw out the image of the tree to the beings and was instantly bombarded with more questions. He began focusing on the image of a lemon being squeezed.

Somewhere in the back of his mind Max knew Michael had called to him. But he was so focused on the questions before him, he could barely conjure up a picture of Michael for himself. It went from fuzzy to foggy to shapeless, then disappeared entirely.

Isabel was sure she could find herself another cleaning project somewhere in the house, but she felt tired. Totally exhausted, actually.

She told herself it was just because she and the others had run around like crazy trying to find Maria's brother. And it wasn't as if they'd been sitting around on their butts before that. They'd been spending every second trying to get Alex back home.

So she really did have more than enough reason to feel wiped out. And the extreme physical sensations—they could have just been caused by stress. She had as much reason to feel stressed as she did to feel tired. More, even.

Isabel ignored the part of her brain that was screaming about the *akino*. She sat down at her desk and flipped on her computer, needing some distraction. When the main screen came up, she clicked on the little icon to bring up her list of favorite places. She didn't feel like shopping. And she'd checked out the Chickclick sites a couple of days ago. Finally her eyes fell on Lucinda Baker's web page. Perfect. Isabel clicked it and waited for it to load.

"I wonder if there's a way that my power could boost the modem speed," she mumbled, impatient to start reading. She tapped her finger against the screen until the photo of Lucinda's face came clear. She clicked on Lucinda's puckered lips, then tapped the screen again until the list of guys' names appeared.

Who had Lucinda been kissing lately? Her eyes were caught by a name that had been highlighted in red—Alex Manes. Lucinda just asked us to say hi for her this afternoon, Isabel thought. She can't have already—

Isabel clicked on Alex's name, tapping the screen with all ten nails. As soon as the first sentences came up, she eagerly began to read.

"Okay, I admit I haven't tried Alexander the Great yet! But don't worry, I will. I hate to admit it, but Stacey Scheinin got to him first. She and Alex had quite the little two-person party by the mall drinking fountain. You all know the one I mean. I got Stacey to give up a few details. Not that it was hard. Stacey and I aren't exactly compadres, but we all know the girl likes to brag. Anyway, Stacey gave Alex the full four tongues. 'He knows what to do, and he does it well,' says Stacey. 'Plus he's adorable.' Is it just me, or has Alex gotten a whole lot yummier since he was dumped by La Isabel?"

"Oh, please." Isabel groaned. But her stomach had clenched so hard, it felt like it was the size of a tennis ball. She knew Lucinda wasn't above making stuff up for her site. But there was no way Lucinda would make up something that made Stacey look good. Saying they weren't compadres was quite the understatement. So Alex and Stacey . . . Isabel shook her head. That just was not right, not after all the mean, catty little things Stacey had said about Alex in the locker room.

Isabel toyed with the idea of posting a response saying exactly that. But it was so not an Isabel move. She would have to—

Suddenly the letters on the screen began to glow. Brighter, brighter, until it hurt to look at them. And still they grew brighter. Isabel closed her eyes, but the light was so strong, it felt like it was penetrating her eyelids.

She fumbled for the computer's off button and finally had to crack open her eyes to find it. Screaming white letters hurtled off the screen. She could feel them penetrating the soft flesh of her eyeballs. The pain was excruciating, and Isabel could do nothing to stop it.

All she could do was cover her face and scream.

FIVE

Michael burst into Isabel's room. "Izzy, what happened? What's wrong?" he demanded.

She screamed again, her hands still pressed tightly to her face. Michael gently pried away her hands and held them in his own. Isabel didn't look up at him. She kept her eyes screwed shut.

"Tell me," he pleaded. He could feel her fingers twitching. "Tell me!" he repeated, forcing some harshness into his voice.

Isabel opened her eyes, but only the tiniest bit, as if she was afraid of what she'd see, then let out a shuddering breath and opened her eyes all the way.

"I'm all right," she said, not quite looking at Michael.

Footsteps pounded down the hall. "Isabel, are you okay?" Mrs. Evans called.

Michael dropped to the floor and wriggled under the bed. Yeah, the Evanses referred to them as their third child, but that didn't mean they'd be happy to see him in Isabel's bedroom at four in the morning.

He heard Isabel's door open. "I had a nightmare,"

53

Isabel explained before her mother could say a word. "I fell asleep at the computer."

Michael heard the mattress squeak above him, and he figured Isabel and her mom had just sat down on the bed.

"Want to tell me about it?" Mrs. Evans asked. "Sometimes that helps."

"I don't . . . I can't remember," Isabel answered.

"That wolf you used to dream about hasn't come back, has he? Because I'm ready for him if he has. I still have a can of the wolf repellent," Mrs. Evans teased.

Michael remembered that wolf repellent. It was a can of hair spray Mrs. Evans had decorated. She'd march into Isabel's room and dewolf it every time Isabel had one of her bad dreams.

"Thanks, Mom," Isabel said. Michael thought he could hear a trace of tears in her voice, and the muscles in his shoulders and neck tensed up. Isabel wasn't a crying kind of girl. "I'm really okay. You should go back to bed," she added.

"You try and get some sleep, too," Mrs. Evans answered. Michael listened as her footsteps crossed the room. He waited until he heard the door close behind her, then he rolled out from under the bed and pushed himself to his feet.

"What happened?" Michael whispered.

"Weren't you listening? I had a nightmare," Isabel whispered back, sounding seriously annoyed.

Michael sat down next to her. "Don't even try to lie to me, Izzy lizard," he said, using the nickname he'd come up with when she was a little girl.

"It's . . . I'm really stressed, okay? And I was reading Lucinda's web page, and I found out that Alex had a make-out session with Stacey. Stacey! I kind of freaked," she explained, tripping over her words. Michael didn't buy it for a second.

"You should have stuck with the nightmare story," he told her. "I mean, the thought of Alex and Stacey together is disgusting—but it would get more of a puking reaction than the scream you let out."

"I don't puke," Isabel informed him with a hint of her usual 'tude.

"Oh, right. What was I thinking?" Michael pushed a damp, sweaty clump of hair behind her ear and studied her face. Her skin had a grayish tint, and she looked like she hadn't slept for days. She looked the way Max had when—

Michael felt like a giant fist had jammed itself into his chest and started squeezing his heart. "It's the *akino*, isn't it?" he asked.

Isabel opened her lips to speak, but no words came out. She simply nodded instead.

She can't end up like Max, Michael thought. He couldn't let that happen. He couldn't lose them both. And Max *was* lost to him, except for little chunks of time here and there. Michael had had to face that just minutes before. He'd stood in front of Max, calling his name, and Max hadn't even known Michael was there.

The hand in his chest had finished with his heart and moved on to his lungs, squeezing until Michael found it hard to breathe.

"What am I going to do?" Isabel asked.

Michael didn't know what to tell her. How to protect her. He wanted to throw back his head and scream in fear and frustration. Yeah, that would make Izzy feel a lot better, he thought, feeling disgusted with himself. He was so lame at this comforting thing. He wished Maria were here. She always knew how to make people feel better, even if it was only with a touch.

Michael struggled to suck some air into his flattened lungs, then reached over and pulled Isabel close to him. He buried his head in her hair. At least he could do that without screwing it up.

"You were supposed to tell me that you'd take care of it," Isabel said, her voice muffled against his shoulder.

The hand began crushing his ribs, sending splinters of bone into Michael's body. He was Izzy's second big brother. He *was* supposed to tell her that he'd take care of it. But if he did, they'd both know it was a lie.

He forced himself to spit out the words that he didn't want to say and that she didn't want to hear.

"Maybe I should get the communication crystals. I don't want you to have to suffer like Max—"

Isabel jerked away from him, her blue eyes dark with emotion. "You want me to connect to the consciousness?" she cried.

"I don't *want* you to. I don't want to have to do it myself. But what choice—," Michael began.

"You said Trevor told you that you won't die if you don't connect to the consciousness. He said that was just what the beings of the consciousness wanted you to believe," Isabel burst out. She jumped up and straightened the already straight row of books on the shelf over her computer.

"As much as I hate to admit it, we don't have a lot of reason to trust Trevor," Michael reminded her. "He said he'd gone through his *akino* without making the connection, but he also said he'd come to Earth to find me. He didn't mention the part about planning to steal the Stone, or finding DuPris, or wanting to kill Max. So basically everything that came out of Trevor's mouth could have been crap."

Isabel whirled back to face him. "The rebellion against the consciousness—if it wasn't led by DuPris, I'd join up in a heartbeat. Maybe Trevor was just waiting to tell you the truth about everything until he knew he could trust you."

"If the rebellion isn't more Trevor bull, maybe there is a way to survive the *akino* without making the connection," Michael said slowly. "It's not like you could rebel while being part of the consciousness. Look at Max. He's a zombie half the—"

Hey, genius. That's probably not exactly helpful to Isabel, Michael told himself.

"He is," Isabel agreed quietly. "And that's why I can't join, even if it means . . ." She let her words trail off, but it wasn't as if they both didn't know what she was about to say—even if it means dying.

Isabel gave him a weak smile. "You should be thanking me," she said. "I'll be the lab rat. If I survive without making the connection, then you'll know it's safe for you to go through your *akino* without it, too."

Michael's stomach turned. This was just so wrong. *He* should be protecting Isabel, making sure it was safe for her.

"Don't be such a guy," Isabel said, catching the look on his face.

"I just . . . I can't stand the thought of you—" Michael couldn't continue. He stared down at the floor, trying to get a grip. If he let himself look at her right now, he'd totally lose it.

"Don't tell anyone, okay?" Isabel asked. "I don't want to be subjected to an intervention or something. Those are so last century."

Michael nodded, eyes still on the floor. "You want me to stay? I can get the sleeping bag."

"No, I'll be all right," Isabel told him. "It's almost morning, anyway."

Michael reluctantly stood up and turned toward the door.

"See you at school tomorrow," she added.

Michael didn't look back. He couldn't.

Adam stepped out of the UFO museum and stared up at the sky. It was gray as cement and seemed lower than it usually was. He hated days like this. It felt like the whole world was part of the underground compound. It felt like the sun was just a figment of his imagination.

Seeing Liz would help. She was better than the sun. Adam knew Michael would crack up if he could hear that thought, but it was true. The sun made Adam feel extra alive, and so did Liz. But somehow Liz was the more powerful energy source.

He pulled the keys out of his pocket and stared at them for a moment before locking the door. It was an amazing feeling—having keys. It was like something actually belonged to him. And he belonged somewhere.

Adam was looking forward to the museum's grand reopening. It would be cool to have people in the place. Adam liked crowds. He liked the feel of the edges of his aura blending with others'. He'd spent enough time alone to last him for the rest of his life. There was no place in the world more lonely than a Project Clean Slate cell. Yes, there were guards posted on him all the time, but that just constantly reminded him of the fact that he was really all by himself.

Adam put his keys back in his pocket, enjoying the weight of them, and wandered down Main Street. It was lunchtime, so nobody would think it was strange for a teenager to be out on the street on a school day.

He'd gone into every one of the little shops many times. He'd even started to get a kick out of all the alien souvenir stuff, which had freaked him out at first. But he didn't feel like hitting them all again. He didn't want to spend any more time under the gray sky than he had to. It gave him the wiggins. That's what Michael called the creepy, pinpricks-on-the-back-of- the-neck feeling—the wiggins.

A bus pulled up to the stop half a block away, and Adam ran for it. He made it just before the doors wheezed closed. "Target again?" the driver asked. Adam gave a sheepish smile. He *did* go to Target more than anybody else in town. There just wasn't that much to do until school got out, and Target was cool.

When the museum reopens, maybe Michael will let me work there during the day, Adam thought. He could rearrange the molecular structure of his face and body so he looked like an adult. It would be his secret identity—like Clark Kent or Peter Parker. Adam shook his head. Another thought that would crack Michael up.

Except that Michael hadn't been cracking up over anything since Trevor took off with DuPris.

Adam leaned his head against the window and stared at the strip malls and fast-food restaurants. When the bus pulled up at the stop in front of Target, he bolted off and raced across the parking lot so he'd have as little time under the sky as possible.

He felt better the moment he was through the electronic doors. Even the smell was somehow comforting—all different variations of clean and new. Adam headed for the long row of magazines, always his first stop. His gaze was snagged by the words on the cover of a women's magazine: *How to Send the Signal That You Want to Be More Than Friends.*

He took a quick look around to make sure that no one was watching—even Adam the mole boy had figured out that guys shouldn't be seen reading *Cosmo*—and found the article as fast as he could. He needed help with the Liz situation because the data he'd gathered so far were somewhat confusing.

Fact: Liz had kissed him. The kiss had been initiated by *her.* This was good.

Fact: Unfortunately, when Liz had initiated the kiss, she'd been in a state of complete emotional chaos. She'd had a fight with her papa that she thought had destroyed their relationship. This was bad.

Fact: The day after Liz had initiated the kiss, she had broken up with Max. This was good.

Fact: Liz had stopped looking Adam in the eye. This was bad.

Fact: Liz had almost stopped looking Max in the eye. Adam wasn't entirely sure how he felt about that.

Adam started reading the article, hoping for some kind of guidance. "Try a red slip or bra," the article suggested. "A flash of red underwear sends a major I'm-looking-for-some-lovin' signal."

He quickly skipped to the second recommendation. "Try dropping something, and take just a few seconds too long when you bend over to pick it up. It's obvious, but guys are dense, so obvious is often necessary."

There was no way this was going to help him figure out if Liz was or could ever be the slightest bit interested in him in a boyfriend kind of way. Adam slapped the magazine shut and stuck it back on the rack. He tried to push out of his mind the image of Liz Ortecho in silky red underwear that set off her dark skin. It didn't feel right to think of her that way.

He quickly headed away from the magazines. His footsteps slowed as he spotted one of the toy aisles out of the corner of his eye. Adam knew he was way too old for toys. He knew that getting caught playing with toys in Target was higher on the humiliation scale than getting caught looking at *Cosmo*. But he'd never gotten to play with toys in the compound. *Dad* Valenti—Adam still cringed when he thought about how he'd grown up thinking Valenti was actually his father—had decided that toys distracted Adam too much from the experiments evaluating his powers.

Adam's brain kept telling him that someone who should be in high school couldn't play with toys, but his feet turned toward them, anyway, and in a few seconds he was sitting on the floor with a remote-controlled robot. He fiddled with the controls until he'd managed to get the robot to march to the end of the aisle and around the corner. He wanted to see if he could get it to circle all the way back to him.

He scooted around so he was facing the direction from which the robot should appear. It didn't.

"The cow says . . . moo," an electronic voice announced from the next aisle. There was a pause, then, "The rooster says . . . cock-a-doodle-doo."

"Do you see a robot over there?" Adam asked. He figured it had to be a little kid playing with the animal toy, so Adam didn't think he had to be too embarrassed.

The little kid didn't answer. The robot didn't appear. "The sheep says . . . baa," the electronic voice stated.

Adam shoved himself to his feet and trotted around to the next aisle. What he saw stopped him cold. Max Evans was sitting cross-legged in the middle of the aisle, holding a brightly colored plastic toy.

"Max!" Adam exclaimed once he got over the surprise. "What are you doing here?"

Max pulled the string on the toy in his hand. "The duck says . . . quack," the electronic voice said.

Adam hurried over and crouched next to Max. His eyes had that unfocused look they got when he'd made a deep connection to the consciousness—something else that gave Adam the creeps. He tapped Max on the shoulder. Max didn't even blink. He just pulled the string again. "The cow says . . . moo," the electronic voice obediently replied.

"Max, uh, shouldn't you be in school?" Adam asked. He hesitated, then gave Max a hard slap on the back. Max started to pull the string again, but Adam pulled the toy away before he had the chance.

Max's eyes fluttered, then slowly focused on Adam. "What are you doing here?" he asked.

Adam shrugged casually, even though his heart was pounding from the weirdness of it all. "I don't know," he said. "Just killing time. What about you?"

A deep line appeared between Max's eyebrows as he looked around the toy aisle. He rubbed his hands over his face. "I . . . man, I don't even remember coming in here. We're in Target, right?"

"Yeah." Adam straightened up, then reached down and helped Max to his feet. "Are you going to, um, head back to school?"

"I guess I . . ." Max's voice trailed off. He picked up a large, fuzzy teddy bear and started to stroke its fur.

He lifted one shoulder at Adam almost apologetically.

"It's a consciousness thing," he explained. "Some of the beings want to know how it feels. I think I'll stay here for a while." He started sounding sort of sleepy. Maybe even drugged.

"Are you sure?" Adam asked. Max's eyes had grown almost as glassy as the bear's.

"Missing a day of school isn't going to hurt me," Max answered.

As Max started to drift off again, his words replayed in Adam's mind. Before he could even blink, he had an amazing idea. A completely amazing, exciting idea.

Liz sucked in her breath as Max walked down the hall toward her. The intensity and focus she saw in his bright blue eyes was almost too much to bear. He was one hundred percent *there*. She could tell not even a fraction of a percent of his attention was on the consciousness or anything else.

It was exactly the way he used to look at her all the time. Liz had a wild impulse to run straight over to him and just hurl herself into his arms. But that wasn't a possibility. She and Max weren't together anymore.

Max smiled as he reached her, one of the smiles that made Liz feel like she was the most beautiful, wonderful, amazing girl ever born.

"Um, hi," she said, an attack of shyness coming over her.

"Liz," he whispered, leaning close, initiating a tiny tremor through her entire body. "It's me. Adam."

Liz's heart slammed in her rib cage, and she backed away a step, feeling a little dizzy. "What?"

"I knew Max wasn't going to be here, so I decided to, you know." Adam made squishing motions in front of his face. "I wanted to see . . . the school. Is it okay?"

"Uh, sure. I guess." She wanted to ask him where Max was and why he wasn't in school, but she had a feeling she didn't really want to know the answer.

"Why not? I'll show you around," Liz told him, struggling to sound like she hadn't just been body slammed. "Come on." She led the way to the cafeteria and pulled open one of the double doors. "This is the caf," she said. "Do you want to get food? We could go sit with—"

"No," Adam answered quickly. "I want to see the rest."

Liz let the door swing shut and led the way down the hall. "These are the lockers," she explained, letting her fingers trail across the green-painted metal, bumping each lock as she walked. "It's where we keep books and stuff." She paused. "This one's mine."

"Can I see inside?" Adam asked, all puppy-dog eager.

"There's not much to see," Liz answered. "But why not?" She began to dial the combination, messed it up, and had to start again. She wondered how long it would have taken her to figure out what was going on if Adam hadn't told her he wasn't Max. A few weeks ago she'd have known almost instantly. But lately she didn't feel like she knew Max down to the bone the way she used to. There were even times where he was a complete stranger to her.

Liz pulled open her locker, revealing a neat row of books, a binder, and a stuffed alien wearing sunglasses that Max had given her as a joke.

"Is this your sister?" Adam asked, lightly touching the photo taped just under the one of her and Max.

"Yeah. That's Rosa," Liz answered. She looked into his eyes. "I never got to—"

This was too strange. She couldn't have this conversation with Adam while he looked like Max.

"Come here for a second." She pulled him up the stairs and down the hall to the little room where all the biology equipment was stored.

"What's that smell?" Adam asked as she shut the door behind him.

"Formaldehyde," she answered, her brain flashing on her and Max making out in this room, joking about how the smell of formaldehyde was a turn-on. "Could you go back to your regular self for a minute?"

Adam began the transformation immediately, without asking why. His hair darkened from blond to light brown, growing finer and silkier. His eyes turned from intense bright blue to leaf green, while his body grew a few inches shorter and lost a little muscle.

"Okay?" he asked when he'd finished.

Liz nodded. "I never got to say thank you for convincing me to go and talk to my papa. You were right. We had this long, amazing talk about Rosa, and we hadn't talked about her since she died. I told him everything, everything I've been wanting to say for years. How he doesn't have to be afraid because I'm not Rosa and nothing bad is going to happen to me." The words came out a little choked, and Adam reached out and gently touched her face.

He's so sweet, she thought, realizing how much she'd come to count on Adam lately. How much it meant to her to have someone look at her the way Adam was looking at her right now—as if there was nothing more important in the whole world.

It felt good. It did.

But it didn't feel the way it had when Max used to look at Liz that way.

Used to. That was the key. The Max Liz was remembering—that Max didn't exist anymore.

SIX

Isabel spotted Alex hanging out in front of the gym with Steve Lydick, Doug Highsinger, Patrick Briscoe, and Josh Martinez.

They can't be responding to Alex's new gorgeousness, she thought as she headed toward them. But they had probably noticed that Alex had snagged the interest of pretty much every girl in school. Because of that, they'd probably decided he was worthy of their company. She rolled her eyes. Guys were such . . . *guys*.

"Miss Isabel," a breathy voice called from behind her. Isabel turned, and Stacey bopped up to her. "If you're thinking about going up to the guys, I thought you might want to borrow some of my blush. And maybe some concealer, too. I wish I had some foundation for you. But I don't need it."

"Thanks, Stacey, but—"

Isabel blanked. Usually it was so easy to come up with the appropriate response to one of Stacey's little digs, but today she was right. I do look like hell, Isabel thought. She'd spent fifteen minutes in a bathroom stall, using her powers on her face, and another ten in front of the mirror, touching up her makeup, and still she had *akino* face—grayish skin, dull eyes, lips that had started to crack a little.

"But what?" Stacey asked.

"But I'm fine," Isabel muttered.

"You don't have much time before you need to get ready for the game!" Stacey reminded her, bopping away without a care in the world.

Isabel didn't bother to answer. She continued toward Alex, relieved when Stacey didn't come along.

"Hey, guys," she said when she'd reached the little crowd. "Can I borrow Alex for a minute?" Without a second glance at anyone in the circle, she took Alex by the arm and led him away.

"Oh, man, Isabel, too?" she heard Patrick complain. *Even when I look bad, I look good,* she thought with satisfaction.

"What's up?" Alex asked when Isabel sat him down on one of the benches in front of the administration office. Isabel noticed him noticing Lucinda Baker as she strutted by.

"I heard you went out with Stacey," Isabel said.

"Yeah." Alex kept his eyes on Lucinda until she was through the main doors. "And?"

"And I don't want you—" Isabel realized she sounded way too possessive. She reminded herself she was talking to a guy she'd broken up with. "Look, you are way too good for Stacey. You

70

don't even want to know the things she used to say about you."

Alex tipped back his head and laughed. "This is just too freakin' bizarre. Isabel Evans is jealous—of me and Stacey Scheinin."

Isabel's sallow skin suddenly felt incredibly hot. "I'm not jealous," she snapped. Alex gave her a yeah-right look that made her blood boil even more, but she managed to keep her outer cool. "We're friends," she continued. "As your friend, I'm saying you could do a lot better."

Alex waved at Maggie McMahon as she passed by.

"Don't even think about it," Isabel warned. "Unless you like the idea of having a girlfriend who makes you dress in the same colors as she does every day."

"So no Stacey. No Maggie. Anybody else?" Alex asked, smirking at her.

"No Lucinda," Isabel answered quickly. Too quickly.

"And you're not jealous?" Alex teased.

"I admit that I kind of liked being the only one who realized how great you were, okay?" Isabel answered. "So, yes, if you have to hear the words, I'm a little jealous. But mostly I just don't want you to end up with someone who doesn't deserve you."

Alex stretched his legs out in front of him. "Now that you've admitted it, I can tell you that I have no plans on going out with Stacey again. She has the brain of an earthworm."

Isabel gave a snort of laughter that turned into a deep, racking cough. She concentrated on breathing, just breathing, until it passed.

"You okay?" Alex asked. But he wasn't looking at her. He was checking his watch. Nice to know you care, Isabel thought.

"Yeah," she answered weakly. She'd felt that cough all the way through her body. Her *hair* was aching from its force.

Alex stood up, but Isabel didn't follow. She wanted to give herself another minute to recover.

"Don't worry, Iz. The girl I'm hooking up with in—" He checked his watch again. "Thirty-four minutes is definitely worthy."

"Who?" Isabel demanded.

Alex grinned at her, his eyes shining. "A college girl. Can you believe that? Alex Manes going out with a college girl. I don't think any of my brothers achieved that when they were in high school."

At least it's not Stacey. Or Maggie. Or Lucinda, Isabel thought. She could not handle the mental picture of any of them with Alex.

"I should go," he told her, backing up a step. "Don't want to be late for my college girl."

"Go." Isabel waved him off with both hands. "Enjoy." She leaned her head back against the wall as she watched him leave, then she slowly rose to her feet.

"Oh, goody, it's almost time to cheer," she muttered, glancing at the hall clock. She headed to the locker room to change into her uniform.

"Hey, Iz," Corrine Williams called as Isabel made her way over to her gym locker. "I hear Alex is going out with some college girl."

"Yeah, we were just talking about that," Isabel answered, trying desperately to sound like her old self. "We both agreed that—other than me—there really isn't a girl in this school who deserves him."

Tish Okabe, Isabel's closest friend on the squad, sent her a semihurt look.

"I didn't mean you," Isabel whispered as she sat down next to Tish on the wooden bench.

"Do you think I, um, might ever have a chance . . . with Alex?" Tish whispered back.

What did that wormhole do to him? Isabel thought. It had to be more than just a little beauty buff up.

She realized Tish was waiting for an answer. "Sure, you have a chance," Isabel said as she opened her locker. She plucked her cheerleading sweater off its hanger, and it slithered out of her fingers. She reached down and picked it up, then immediately dropped it again.

Isabel flexed her fingers, trying to get rid of the

tiny tremor buzzing through them. How much longer do I have? she wondered. How much longer before the *akino* is at full force?

Maria took a peek at Michael out of the corner of her eye, pretending she was still watching the basketball game. He's still totally messed up, she thought. Actually, he seemed even worse than he had right after he discovered the Trevor-DuPris connection.

Something else had happened. Something new. And the king of I-can-handle-my-own-problems wasn't talking. Maria felt like smacking him.

Adam climbed up the bleachers to their row, balancing four big sodas in his hands. Maria and Michael each took one, Michael immediately adding hot sauce from the little packets he always had on him.

"Thanks," Maria murmured, noting that Adam's fingers lingered on Liz's when he handed her her soda, noting that Liz didn't pull away. It had been clear since almost the first moment Adam saw Liz that he was gaga. But lately Maria got the feeling that Liz was getting a little gaga back. Well, maybe not gaga. Maybe not even *ga*. Still, every once in a while Maria caught a flicker of interest from Liz toward their little Adam.

Maria didn't blame her, although it seemed so wrong that after all Liz and Max had gone through together . . . she shook her head. There was no point in thinking about that now. Max was a whole other issue.

"What the hell is wrong with you, Lydick?" Michael exploded.

Projection, Maria thought. Yeah, Steve Lydick had missed a shot that should have been a swish, but Michael had yelled like Steve had personally offended him or something.

Maria slid a little closer and put her hand on Michael's arm. It was either that or smack him. He didn't acknowledge the fact that she was touching him, but she felt his muscles relax a little. Sometimes the only comfort Michael would allow was physical. Maria had no problem with touching him, except for the part where she was tortured by wanting to touch him a lot more. She just wished he would *talk* to her. He wasn't going to start feeling any better if he didn't let whatever was putrefying in him out.

The band started to play, announcing the start of halftime. "Want to go outside and get some air?" she asked Michael. "It smells like a gym in here."

"I want to watch Izzy do her cheer," Michael answered. Keeping focused on the court.

"We have time," Maria urged, giving his arm a little squeeze. "Unless you really need to hear the patriotic songs medley again."

"Nah. You go if you want. I'm going to stay

here." He pulled his arm away from her hand. She had to give him points for trying to be a little subtle about it—he did the head-scratch-arm-pull thing. But Maria knew that her touch had started to irritate him.

Maybe I should read one of those books on massaging auras, she thought. That could be a way to covertly do something for Michael. She didn't need to see auras to know that his was seriously out of whack. It probably had one of those purple grief nets. Plus a whole lot of anger splotches.

"Hey, Maria," Liz called over the loud brass solo section of the medley. "I just found out Adam doesn't have a birthday—or, you know, a day he celebrates as his birthday. They didn't give him one in the compound. You're the astrology guru. What do you think it should be?"

Maria was grateful for a little distraction. "Hmmm. How would you describe Adam?" she asked Liz, curious to hear the answer.

Liz studied Adam for a moment, and a blush began to creep up his neck. She better look away before he achieves meltdown, Maria thought.

"I'd say Adam is empathetic, intelligent, and sweet," Liz answered.

Interesting. Liz definitely didn't seem to be ga-ish over Adam. But it did sound like she liked him a lot and like she saw him as someone safe, someone who

76

would never break her heart. Maria could see why that could appeal to Liz right now.

"I hope you're not going to stand for that," Michael told Adam. "Never let a girl call you sweet. It means they think you have no—"

"Don't worry. No one's ever going to call you sweet," Maria told Michael. Although deep down in the core of him, Maria suspected Michael was one of the sweetest people around. No one cared more about the people he loved than Michael, not that he'd admit he loved anybody at all.

"So what am I?" Adam asked.

"I'd say you're a Pisces, a sweet dream boy," Maria answered. "So you could pick any day between February nineteenth and March twentieth."

"When's your birthday, Liz?" Adam said. Michael gave a snort of derision, and Maria gave in to her impulse to smack him.

"May sixteenth," Liz answered. She released her long, dark hair from its ponytail and let it fall around her shoulders.

"I want to be March sixteenth," Adam announced. Maria shot Michael a warning look. He ignored her and rolled his eyes.

"So whipped," Michael muttered, but not loud enough for Adam to hear.

"You are definitely a Sagittarius in one big way," Maria said in his ear. "You're completely tactless."

"You don't even know when my birthday is," Michael shot back.

"December twentieth," Maria said, causing Michael to narrow his eyes at her. "At least that's the day social services chose for you," Maria said, a little too quickly.

"And you know this because?" Michael prodded.

"I asked Max once," Maria answered lamely.

Michael raised his eyebrow, and his mouth twisted into a conceited smile. Maria thought she was going to have to smack him again, but the medley wrapped up, and the cheerleaders trotted onto the polished wood floor of the basketball court.

"Go, Isabel!" Maria cried, clapping.

The cheerleaders launched into a new routine, one that was half what you'd see on a dance floor and half what you'd see during a gymnastics meet. Isabel was perfectly in sync as she did a double back flip, but when she came out of it, Maria couldn't help noticing that she looked exhausted. All of her usual Isabel-goddess-glow was gone.

Maria reached around Adam and nudged Liz. "Does Isabel look okay to you?" she asked as the cheerleaders began to form a pyramid.

Liz didn't answer. Her eyes were locked on the cheerleaders, her expression grim. Maria jerked her gaze over to them. Isabel stood in the top position. And she was teetering ever so slightly.

Maria grabbed Michael's hand, holding her breath. The gym went perfectly silent.

Isabel repositioned her feet slightly. She raised her arms. She smiled.

She's going to be all right, Maria thought.

But a moment later Isabel plummeted to the floor. Maria let out a loud gasp along with the rest of the spectators and jumped to her feet. Then the entire place became eerily silent.

Isabel was splayed out on the floor.

And she wasn't moving.

SEVEN

"I'm not saying it again. It was Stacey's fault. She was wobbly, so I was wobbly, and that's why I fell," Isabel repeated. She picked a tiny piece of dead skin off her lower lip, and a droplet of blood appeared.

Max glanced around Michael and Adam's living room. Michael, Adam, Liz, and Maria were all looking at Isabel with varying degrees of disbelief. Clearly no one was buying her story completely. Max sure as hell wasn't.

"I wasn't even hurt. Just let it go already," Isabel added. She licked the droplet of blood away.

A cluster of beings in the consciousness shot Max a question about a cartoon on the muted TV. Max ignored it, forcing his connection to the consciousness as low as it would go. He needed to concentrate on his sister.

"Okay, so you fell, and you weren't hurt. Fine," Max said. "But what about the rest of it—the cracked lips, the way your face is all pale?"

"Oh, God. You sound exactly like Michael," Isabel exclaimed, burying her face in her hands.

Max glared over at Michael. "You know something you aren't saying?" he demanded. But he didn't even need Michael to answer. His aura said it all. There were sickly yellow snakes of fear all through it.

I should have seen it before, Max thought. No, forget that. He shouldn't have needed to see anything in Michael's aura. One good look at Isabel should have told him everything he needed to know.

"It's the *akino*," he said flatly.

"Whether it is or it isn't is my business," Isabel shot back, her voice suddenly stronger. "It isn't open for group discussion."

Maybe he should have caught it earlier, but there was still time to do what needed to be done. Max pushed himself up from the floor. He strode over to Isabel and pulled her to her feet. "We're going home," he said firmly. "I'm getting the communication crystals, and you're making the connection to the consciousness."

Isabel jerked away her arm, blue eyes burning feverishly. "No."

That's all she said. Just "no." But the threads of gunmetal gray crisscrossing her aura told him that she had no intention of backing down.

Max's gaze flicked briefly to the TV screen. The beings were more insistent now, pushing him to give the cartoon his whole attention so they could experience it.

82

Not now! Max thought. He ordered his eyes back to Isabel. "Izzy, if you don't—" His eyes sought out the TV again. He gave up, allowing the beings to watch the cartoon while he continued to talk to his sister. "If you don't connect, you'll die.. I know. It almost happened to me. I was in the tunnel of light. Another few seconds and I'd have been gone."

Liz leaned over and snapped off the TV. "Thanks," Max told her. She didn't respond. She didn't even look at him.

"Maybe Max is right," Michael said, shoving his hands into the pockets of his jeans.

"Maybe? Maybe!" Max exploded. "There's no maybe about it."

"Hey, Trevor said—," Michael began.

"Trevor? As in the guy who tried to kill me?" Max snapped, his ire raising at an alarming rate. "That's who you're—" Another cluster of beings in the consciousness prodded Max, wanting to know what the smell coming from Adam was. Max ignored the question. "That's who you're going to listen to?"

"And who are we listening to right now, Max?" Isabel demanded, narrowing her eyes. "Is that you talking or a million little voices in your head?"

"Not that bull again," Max burst out, his hands clenching into fists. "All of you have this idea that I'm not myself anymore just because I'm connected to the consciousness."

83

"You're not you," Isabel told him, tears welling up in her eyes. "My brother Max would never have been watching cartoons while he was talking to me about the possibility that I might die." Her last words came out as a shriek.

"She's right," Liz said from her spot on the floor. She wrapped her arms tighter around her knees, as if preparing to ward off a blow. "You are—were— the most caring, considerate person I'd ever met. You couldn't even walk past a mouse in the bio lab if you knew it was in pain. Remember that day you healed that mouse, Fred?" This time Liz met his gaze steadily. "I think that was the day I fell in love with you."

The beings blasted another question about the Adam smell. Max scrubbed his face with his fingers. "Adam, what kind of gum are you chewing?"

"One piece banana. One piece cinnamon," Adam answered, without blinking an eye.

"Do you even listen to yourself, Max?" Michael burst out. "We're talking about Isabel's life, and you're babbling about bubble gum."

Max sat down on the floor again and closed his eyes, trying to block out as much sensation as possible so the consciousness would have less to respond to.

"I don't know what Trevor's deal is," Max said through gritted teeth. "I don't know why he'd say it's possible to survive the *akino* without making the connection. But I experienced it. I'm the only one of us who has." He took a deep breath and emphasized every word, hoping they would take him seriously. "It. Can. Not. Be. Survived."

"I remember standing by your bed near . . . near what we thought was the end," Maria jumped in. "Remember? We didn't just think Max was going to die—we thought he *had* died. He actually stopped breathing."

Max opened his eyes just a touch and peered up at Isabel. "Are you listening?" he asked, then he closed his eyes again, resisting the urge to run his fingers across the plastic of the closest beanbag chair to allow the beings of the consciousness to feel it.

"If I have to choose between dying or being like Max is now, I'd rather die," Isabel spat out.

"Don't say that," Maria exclaimed.

"I don't think it sounds too bad to be part of the consciousness," Adam said matter-of-factly. "You'd never be alone."

"You'd be a puppet," Isabel cried. "And you know what that feels like, right, Adam? You killed Valenti while you were—"

"It's not the same," Max protested, keeping his eyes closed. "The consciousness doesn't make me kill. It doesn't—"

"It tried to make you kill DuPris," Liz reminded him, voice harsh. "You might not always be a puppet. But the consciousness can pull your strings whenever."

Max heard footsteps pass in front of him. "Isabel, you have to do it," he heard Maria say. He risked a brief squint and saw that Maria had wrapped Isabel in her arms. "I can't lose my frister," she added.

"What's a frister?" Adam asked.

"It's more than a friend, almost a sister," Liz answered. She sprang to her feet and joined the Isabel-Maria knot.

"Listen to them," Max begged. "If you can't listen to me, listen to them." He felt like he'd swallowed something alive, something with claws. It tore at his guts as he waited to hear Isabel's response.

"If I join the consciousness, you *will* lose me," Isabel explained. "If I take the risk, if I go through the *akino* without making the connection, you might lose me. But I might survive. At least I'll have the *chance* of surviving."

"I'm not dead!" Max yelled. He couldn't sit there another second, doing nothing while his sister talked about him this way—as if he'd killed himself. He jumped up, pushed his way between Liz and Maria, and grabbed both of Isabel's hands in his.

"What are you doing?" Isabel cried.

"I'm going to show you the consciousness. I'm

going to prove that it's nothing to be afraid of," Max answered.

Isabel tried to jerk away when she realized he had begun making the connection with her. Max tightened his grip. He wasn't going to let her go. He was never going to let her go.

Images from Isabel began to flash through Max's mind. A silvery incubation pod, broken open. A dark-haired guy on a motorcycle. A creature that was half Sheriff Valenti and half wolf. Max's face, eyes vacant, mouth slack.

And he was in. He could feel Isabel's heart beating in his body now. *Their* body. He could feel her breath in his lungs.

As slowly as he could, he allowed the volume of his connection to the consciousness to come back up and slid into the ocean of auras.

He felt a flicker of panic from Isabel as they were surrounded by the billions of beings, as they became part of the one, the whole, the single living entity— made up of many—that was the consciousness.

The panic in Isabel swelled. Her—*their*—heartbeat began to flutter. Faster. Faster.

Abruptly his connection with Isabel broke. Max's heart caught with fear. He reached for her, but all he felt was blackness.

"I can't even describe how it felt," Isabel said. She pulled her comforter tighter around her shoulders, even though Michael felt it was a little too warm in her bedroom already.

"It's like I was . . . dissolving," she continued, her eyes wide. "Or like I was being swallowed up. Then I guess I fainted. I've never fainted in my life."

Lightning bolts of yellow fear zigzagged across her aura as she spoke. And when she glanced over at the communication crystals on her bedside table, her entire aura became the color of fear. The yellow light surrounding her gave her face a corpselike appearance.

"I probably would have fainted, too," Michael told her. He rubbed the back of his neck, trying to force all the little hairs back down. What she'd described sounded a lot like death to him. Wasn't that what death was—complete loss of self?

A loud knock sounded at the door, and before he or Isabel could answer, Max came in and stood awkwardly at the foot of Isabel's bed.

"I just wanted to see if you were okay," he said.

"You should have thought about that before you forced me into the connection," Isabel told him, her voice cold enough to turn lava to ice.

"I didn't know it would make you feel so—," Max told her.

"So much like I was *dying*?" Isabel interrupted.

Max picked a little glass kitten off her dresser and turned it over in his hands.

"Most of the time for me, it's like a tropical ocean, with lots of salt in the water, so that you're really buoyant," Max explained. "Sometimes you hit a bad stretch—like a riptide, I guess. But most of the time . . ." He raised the kitten to his lips and licked one of its glass ears. Michael's stomach turned just watching him. "I really thought you'd see that it was nothing to be so afraid of."

"What are you doing to that thing?" Michael burst out.

Max's eyebrows drew together. "I was just looking at it. So?"

"You were *licking* it," Michael informed him, his face a mask of disgust. His best friend was getting freakier by the second.

Max put the kitten down fast but didn't offer any explanation.

"Let me guess. Some of the beings wondered how it tasted?" Isabel asked.

"I just wanted to be sure you were okay," Max said. He gave the communication crystals a pointed look. "You should use those before the pain gets too bad." He glanced from Isabel to Michael and seemed to tense up. Then he hurried out of the room, shutting the door behind him.

Probably afraid he'd start licking something else and totally push Isabel off the sanity cliff, Michael thought.

"I feel like I don't even have a brother anymore,"

Isabel whispered, staring at the closed door.

Don't go there, Michael ordered himself. If he started thinking about what Max had become, Michael would go flying off the sanity cliff himself. He had to concentrate on Isabel.

"You know if I—*when* I—get too weak to stop him, he's going to force those crystals into my hand," Isabel said, sounding like a small child. "He'll make me connect whether I want to or not. Maria and Liz would probably even help him. Maybe even Alex, too, if he was through sampling every girl in the state," Isabel added, still staring at the door.

Michael reached out and took her chin between his fingers. He forced her to look at him. "I'm not letting anybody do anything to you that you don't want done."

Was it right to promise her that? Was it right to agree to help her do something that could possibly kill her? Michael didn't know for sure, but it was necessary. Isabel needed someone on her side, someone who'd go with her through hell and back if that's what she wanted.

Michael had to be that guy. Right or wrong, he was seeing this thing through with her.

"I don't know if you'll be able to stop him," Isabel said. "Not if he gets everyone else on his side. Unless—"

Suddenly her expression became determined,

and she looked more like the Isabel he knew and loved than she had in the last few days. She threw off the comforter and swung her legs around so they were hanging off the bed.

"Unless we leave," she said. "Now."

Michael froze. "Are you sure?"

"I'm sure," Isabel said. "If Max can't find me, I'm safe."

EIGHT

Trevor's stomach convulsed as he broke the connection with DuPris. He pulled in a deep breath and blew it out hard, trying to get his revulsion under control. Necessary sacrifices, he told himself. Necessary. Sacrifices. He took another breath, blew it out, then realized DuPris was staring at him with a mix of amusement and condescension.

"My human body still has responses that are difficult to control," Trevor muttered. At least the responses to images of torture and destruction are tough, he thought.

"They are an extremely sensitive race," DuPris commented. "In an episode of *Laverne and Shirley,* Laverne actually stopped speaking to Shirley just because she thought Shirley was too friendly to her boyfriend."

"Uh, I didn't see that one," Trevor answered.

"I have it on tape," DuPris answered. He picked the purple-green Stone of Midnight off the coffee table and cradled it in his hand. "It's going to reach full strength even earlier than I hoped. Two more charging sessions and we should be there."

Two more. You can deal with two more, Trevor told himself. He rubbed his sweaty palms on the sides of his jeans, hoping DuPris wouldn't notice. There were dozens of members of the Kindred—no, more than that, *hundreds*—who had desperately wanted to join DuPris on Earth and work side by side with the rebel leader. Trevor had been chosen because of his relationship with Michael, but he was determined to prove that he would have been the best-possible choice under any circumstances. It was his destiny to destroy the consciousness, to finish the crusade that had been so important to his parents, the crusade they had given their lives for.

"I want to get some more work done on the ship today." DuPris began to teleport before Trevor had a chance to respond, clearly assuming that he would follow.

Trevor concentrated on the deserted warehouse they were using for a hangar and allowed his molecules to loosen and then disperse. He welcomed the blackness that overcame him as his brain scattered.

When his body re-formed, DuPris had already begun repairing one of the bashed-in sections of the ship. Trevor chose a deep crater at the opposite end of the craft to work on. He still didn't feel that comfortable around DuPris. With every move Trevor made, every word he spoke, he felt that he was being judged by the leader, judged and found to be somehow lacking.

At least he'd managed not to puke after their connections. It wasn't much to be proud of. But it was something.

Trevor rested his hands on the crater and focused on moving the molecules back into the correct positions. The metal of the ship was usually extremely adaptable, able to shift from solid to near liquid with minimal energy use, allowing for both strength and flexibility. But the molecules of the metal had been coded with a block that made manipulating them almost impossible for any being not connected to the consciousness.

Trevor strained to push all extraneous thoughts out of his head. Thoughts of Michael. Of his parents. Of the nearness of DuPris. Only the molecules, he ordered himself. If he was going to get past the block, it would take every neuron of his human brain.

Slowly the molecules came into focus. He could see them vibrating, see that the metal was in reality billions of separate entities. Trevor began to trace one of the molecules with his mind, searching for anything that felt off, anything that could tell him exactly how the block was coded. He examined the individual atoms and the bonds of positive and negative attraction that bound them together.

Everything appeared normal. So he moved on to the next molecule, scanning the atoms, their protons, electrons, neutrons, and quarks. Normal. On to the next. Normal. And the next. Normal.

Trevor felt frustration begin to build inside him. It could take the rest of his life just to examine the molecules in this one small bashed-in section of the ship.

He clamped down on the emotion—hard. He could allow no distractions. If his attention wavered even for a flicker, he could miss the code. He returned to his examination. Normal. Normal. Normal. Normal.

A dull ache started up behind his eyes. Trevor ignored it. Normal. Normal. Normal. Normal. Normal.

The ache sharpened into a knife of pain, stabbing him in the same spot again and again. Trevor risked a quick glance at DuPris. The leader had his attention on the ship. You don't stop until he stops, Trevor told himself.

The pain moved deeper into his head, but Trevor continued his work. Normal. Normal. Normal. Normal. He gritted his teeth to keep from crying out. Normal. Normal. Normal.

"Take a break if you need one," DuPris called. Trevor shot another glance at him and saw that he was lying on the floor.

Trevor's fingers trembled as he pulled them off the metal. He lowered himself to the ground and stretched out on his back, the pain dulling almost immediately.

"Couldn't we use the power of the fully charged Stone of Midnight for this job?" he asked.

DuPris didn't answer, and Trevor's blood immediately ran cold with fear. He turned his head to look at the leader. The cold expression in his green eyes made it clear that suggestions from Trevor were not going to be tolerated. Trevor forced himself to continue to meet DuPris's gaze. He didn't want the leader to sense any weakness in him.

"When the second Stone is charged and the ship is repaired, you will return home, bringing the Stone with you," DuPris announced.

I've failed, Trevor thought. He's seen my emotions go out of control when we connect, and he has decided he wants—

"You will select a squadron of soldiers from members of the Kindred," DuPris continued.

Trevor blinked, and relief flooded through him. DuPris still planned to give him a role in the rebellion. He hoped his near giddy happiness didn't show on his face.

"The squadron will escort you to the consortium chamber where the third Stone of Midnight is kept," DuPris continued, turning his head to stare up at the cracked and dusty ceiling of the warehouse. "You will instruct the freedom fighters to kill anyone who tries to stop you. You must make sure your squadron is big enough and well armed enough that no matter what the losses, the squadron will be able to get you inside the chamber."

"That's a suicide mission," Trevor burst out before he could censor himself. DuPris's plan would involve thousands of deaths. "Couldn't there be a . . . a more covert—"

"You will follow orders. So will those you command," DuPris answered, voice harsh.

Trevor's mouth snapped shut as his heart dropped. Why couldn't he seem to keep his idiot thoughts unspoken? He pushed himself to his feet.

"Yes, Leader," he said firmly, looking DuPris in the eye. He moved back into position in front of the ship, even though the pain in his head had returned full force the moment he stood up. He placed his hands on the metal, wanting to show DuPris that he was more than eager, more than willing—

To lead thousands to their deaths. The thought screamed through Trevor's head unbidden.

If that's what it takes, he told himself. If that is the sacrifice that is necessary, then it will be done.

Behind him, DuPris began to whistle. He paused for a moment. "Join me," he called to Trevor.

Trevor didn't turn around. He kept his eyes on the ship. "I don't know that song," he answered.

"Theme to the *Andy Griffith Show*," DuPris answered. "One of the best theme songs, second only perhaps to the one for *Gilligan's Island*." He began to whistle again.

Trevor swallowed hard. Less than a minute ago DuPris was planning the deaths of thousands of the Kindred, and now . . .

Now he was whistling?

What kind of being was—

Trevor forced the thought away before he could complete it.

Liz heard her papa's steps slow in front of her door. She smiled as they continued on. He hadn't checked on her. He was really trying to show her that he trusted her, that he knew she wasn't Rosa and he didn't have to be afraid she would die from an overdose the way her sister had.

She rolled onto her side and straightened the rumpled covers. She'd been having a good dream before the sound of the footsteps woke her up. What was it? Something about her and Maria at the community swimming pool? Not quite that.

It wasn't an Adam dream—that's all Liz knew for sure. She also had to admit that she was a little disappointed that it hadn't been an Adam dream.

Every once in a while Adam slipped into her dream orb and created something wonderful for her. Those little encounters with Adam, away from the group, away from real life, were magic.

Liz gazed at the phone on her bedside table. She could just call Adam up and invite him into her dream. She'd never done that before, but she could.

Except that would be encouraging Adam to hope that there could be something more between them. She knew he wanted that. She could see it on his face every time he looked at her.

"And I don't want that," she whispered, needing to hear the words aloud.

Except if she didn't want that, why was she lying there thinking about Adam in the middle of the night? Liz reached for the phone, then hesitated, hand frozen in midair.

There's nothing wrong with wanting to spend a little time with Adam, she thought. It's fun. Fun is good. Hardly anything is fun anymore. It didn't have to be some big deal. It didn't have to be leading somewhere. And if she kept things light and friendly, Adam wouldn't get the wrong idea.

Liz snatched up the phone and dialed, hoping Michael wouldn't be the one who answered. She smiled as she heard Adam's voice say, "Hello."

"It's Liz," she told him. "Do you want to come out and play? I mean, do you want to meet up on the dream plane for a while?"

There was a moment of silence, and Liz's palms started to sweat. "We don't have to," she added quickly.

"No. No! I want to. Definitely," Adam exclaimed. "Just go to sleep, and I'll be there." He hung up without saying good-bye.

Liz hung up the phone and settled back down into her pillows, searching for the most comfortable position. It didn't take too long before she began to feel the drifty, floaty, almost asleep sensations.

And then she was in the science lab, a titration experiment in front of her.

"Do you dream about school a lot?" Adam asked from behind her.

She turned and smiled at him. "At least it's not the one where I'm taking a test naked," she answered. A faint blush colored Adam's cheeks. Liz didn't even want to know where his thoughts had just taken him. "So what are we going to do? Are we going to be goldfish again? That was fun."

"Whatever you want," Adam told her. "You tell me, and I'll make it happen."

"Anything?" Liz twisted her hair into a knot on the top of her head. "That's too hard. Too many choices."

"Well . . . what's your favorite color?" Adam asked.

"Emerald green," Liz answered immediately. Then she realized that was her favorite because it was the rich, vibrant color of Max's aura. "No, pink," she said.

And the entire lab went pink. All shades. Fuchsia. Raspberry. Cherry. Strawberry. Bubble gum. Rose petal. Cotton candy. Only Liz and Adam retained their original coloring.

Liz spun in a circle. "It's like we're inside a . . . I don't know. A bottle of pinkness."

Adam laughed. "Very scientific," he teased. "Now, what's your favorite flavor?"

"Peppermint," Liz answered. Adam picked up a pencil from the lab table and held it up to her lips.

"Bite," he instructed.

Liz took a tiny nibble, and the sharp, sweet taste of peppermint flooded her mouth. She picked up the closest beaker and, grinning at Adam, took a sip of the baby pink liquid inside. "Yum."

"Okay, I know the lab is one of your favorite places. But choose someplace else, someplace you've always wanted to go," Adam told her, his leaf green eyes appearing even more striking amid all the pink.

"A big city. Someplace as not-Roswell as you can get." Liz took another sip of the liquid peppermint, thinking about it. "New York City," she decided. "Top of the Empire State Building." And poof!

They were there. Liz stared at the pink skyscrapers, so tall, they almost touched the pink clouds. "That one over there—that's the Chrysler Building," she told Adam.

"Hey, do you think I grew up underground or something?" Adam joked. "I read all about New York on the web."

"It needs people," Liz said, leaning over the railing and staring down at the street below.

"Up here with us?" Adam sounded surprised and a little disappointed.

"No, down there. Little ant people rushing around doing important New York City things." Almost as soon as the words were out of her mouth, the street was filled with pink people striding purposefully along with pink briefcases and portfolios. "All this pink is making me dizzy," Liz admitted.

And the whole world turned blue. Navy. Sky. Powder. Blueberry. Turquoise. Cobalt.

"Better?" Adam asked. He didn't let Liz answer before he zapped everything yellow.

"Aaah! Too bright!" Liz cried.

Instantly everything went velvety black. Then a double fistful of stars appeared in the sky and a brilliant full moon. Each of the buildings took on a gentle glow.

"This is so beautiful," Liz whispered. "It's perfect."

"Not quite," Adam said.

Liz glanced at him. That's all it took for her to know he wanted to kiss her.

And she wanted to kiss him, too. She did. This setting was so romantic—it all but shouted for a kiss.

Liz looked into his face and realized it wasn't just the setting. It was Adam, too. Sweet Adam with his eager eyes, eyes that looked at Liz as if she was something rare and special.

But as romantic as the setting was, as sweet as Adam was, the time wasn't right.

"It's absolutely perfect just the way it is," she insisted, turning her gaze back toward the city stretched out in front of them. "Thank you, Adam."

NINE

"I thought I'd be the last one here," Max said as he sat down at the usual cafeteria table. "Some of the beings wanted—" He stopped abruptly when he saw Liz's expression fall and her eyes go hard. "Where's Alex?" he asked abruptly.

"Alex is actually here—in the cafeteria here—just not *here* here," Maria told him. She gave him a sympathetic smile, but at the same time she seemed to be watching him for a sign or something. A sign that he wasn't *him* or whatever.

Max glanced around the cafeteria. He almost missed Alex entirely because he was surrounded by girls, most of them in heavy flirt mode.

"I guess we can all see why he decided not to join us," Max said, dropping his backpack down on the empty chair next to him.

Maria snorted. "We can certainly all see what a big idiot he's being. I mean, where's the gratitude? Did those girls bring him back from another planet? I don't think so."

"Actually, neither did we," Max reminded her.

"But we tried!" Maria shot back. She opened a tiny

porcelain box and pulled out two of her hand-blended vitamins. "And he—"

"He's just having some fun," Liz cut in. "What's wrong with that?"

"What's wrong is that we have a situation going," Maria answered. She swallowed the vitamins dry. "And he should be a part of dealing with it."

"How is Isabel doing?" Liz asked Max, her dark brown eyes serious.

Max's heart skipped just from hearing Liz address him, but he pushed the feeling aside. "I'm the last person who would know," Max told her.

Man, he'd screwed up with Izzy. Forcing her to experience the consciousness had made things between them so much worse. And all he was trying to do was keep her alive.

He pulled his lunch out of his backpack. A group of beings were clamoring for the AstroNut bar. They'd become addicted to the candy. Almost anytime Max ate anything, that group would start demanding an AstroNut.

Max dug through his lunch bag and found the candy and a couple of packets of spicy brown mustard. He quickly applied the mustard to the chocolate before the addicts could start a riot. "Do you think Isabel talked Michael into going to the taco stand or something?" he asked, glancing at Maria and Liz. "Both of them would probably rather not look at my face while they're eating."

He couldn't stop the bitterness from seeping into his voice. Isabel and Michael were acting like he was the enemy now. Even Liz was—

The beings were smelling the AstroNut through Max. And they wanted it. Now. He obediently took a bite and was lost to the tastes exploding through his mouth and the beings' reaction to them.

After he swallowed and managed to turn down the volume on the consciousness a little, he realized that Liz and Maria were staring at him.

"What?" he asked.

"We were just saying that neither of us has seen Michael or Isabel all day," Liz told him impatiently. "What about you? Have you seen either of them?"

"No, I haven't," he said. It wasn't that strange for Michael to skip school. But Isabel always showed up. The queen had to let the subjects adore her, as she'd always say.

Where *are* they? he wondered, his bones suddenly feeling like sticks of ice. He glanced at the clock over the back doors. There was still time to check some of the usual spots before the end of the period. Max started to gather his things and stand up. Something could really be wrong. He had to—

Suddenly the volume on the consciousness went up, the beings demanding more AstroNut. Max fell back into his chair and took another bite.

*　　*　　*

When Adam opened the door and saw Liz standing there, his heart shot up to the base of his throat, beating frantically.

"Have you seen Isabel or Michael today?" Liz asked. "Neither of them showed up at school."

He studied her face quickly, trying not to look like he was studying it. Had Liz only come over here to find out about Michael and Isabel? Or had she wanted to see him? Because if she only wanted to know about Michael and Isabel, she could have just called. So maybe she *did*—

"Adam?"

"Haven't seen them," he answered, refocusing on the subject at hand. "Michael didn't come home last night, either." He stepped back so Liz could come inside.

"What?" Liz exclaimed, stepping into the room. "Why didn't you tell someone?"

"He doesn't always come home," Adam said as he closed the door behind her. "I didn't think—" Adam paused, taking in the upheaval in Liz's aura. "I guess it was stupid of me."

Liz shook her head and sighed. "No, it wasn't," she said. "Not if it's normal for him to stay out. Max is the one who should have been on this. He couldn't even remember if Isabel had been home in the morning before school."

Large splotches of anger appeared in her aura along with dark streaks of sadness.

Adam was pretty sure he knew the source of the sadness. It had just hit Liz again how un-Max-like Max had become. She still loved him. Even though he could see that most of the time Liz hated to be in the same room with Max, she still loved him with every molecule in her body. He wondered if she realized that.

And you just have to suck it up, he told himself, using another Michael expression. It was insane to think the mole boy could ever have a girl like Liz, anyway.

"What do you think Michael and Isabel—" Adam was interrupted by a loud knock on the door that made Liz jump slightly. Adam opened it to find Kyle Valenti standing on the staircase that led up from the museum parking lot. Kyle strode in without waiting to be asked.

"I need to know where DuPris is," Kyle announced, hands on hips. He was out of breath, and his face appeared red from exertion. "Once I know where he is, I can handle him, but I don't know how to track him."

"Kyle, go home," Liz said firmly. "And don't even think about going after DuPris. He is more dangerous than—"

"He killed my father," Kyle shouted, his hands fisted by his sides. "I can't just do nothing. Don't you get that? Now tell me where he is."

"We don't know," Liz answered. Adam was glad

she was there to do the talking. Kyle was more than a little bit intimidating.

"You don't know," Kyle repeated, crossing his arms over his chest. "Well, look out the window, and maybe you'll see something that will help you remember."

Liz rushed to the window, and Adam followed right behind her. Down in the parking lot were a cluster of people, two of them with video cameras.

"Reporters," Liz said.

"That's right, braniac," Kyle answered, sounding smug. "If you don't tell me where DuPris is, then I'm going to go back down there and tell *them* all about your friends." He jerked his thumb at Adam. "Starting with that one. I'm sure they'll have a lot of questions for him."

If Michael was here, he'd know what to do. He'd find a way to make Kyle back down. But all Adam could think about was that as soon as the reporters knew where he was, he'd end up back underground somewhere—and the thought paralyzed him.

"You know what? Adam was just saying how he wished he could get on TV," Liz told Kyle.

She reached out and took Adam's hand, but he barely felt it. Usually it would be all he could feel if Liz touched him, but at the moment he was numb.

"Come on, Adam," Liz continued. "Let's go make you a star. I bet we can even get you some endorsement gigs. Maybe one for a fancy toaster or something."

She gave his hand a reassuring squeeze that brought him slightly back to earth.

"Sure. Let's go," Adam managed to say. The reporters terrified him, but he trusted Liz.

"You're bluffing," Kyle said.

Liz didn't reply. She just headed for the door. Adam didn't try to pull away. He let her lead him outside and down the staircase and even got his lips to approximate a smile as the cameras swung toward him.

"The guy's one of the ones I told you about," Kyle yelled from behind them. "He's an alien. And there are three more that I know about. Their names are—"

"You're all from Albuquerque, right?" Liz interrupted.

She knows what she's doing, Adam told himself. Don't freak. Do not freak in front of the reporters. It will only make them suspicious. But all he really wanted to do was run as fast as his human legs would carry him.

"That's right," one of the reporters answered.

"I knew you weren't from Roswell. Everyone in Roswell knows—" She hesitated, shooting a look at Kyle.

"Knows what?" the same reporter asked.

"She's going to give you some load of bull," Kyle warned.

Liz leaned closer to the reporter she'd started the

exchange with. "That's Kyle Valenti. Valenti. Ring a bell? He's the son of the man who used to be sheriff."

"The one who disappeared," the reporter finished, eyes wide.

"Exactly," Liz continued somberly. "Kyle thinks an alien killed his father." She lowered her voice. "It's very sad. He's gone through so much."

"What?" Kyle yelled, storming toward the little crowd. "What did she say to you?"

"Just giving us a little background information," the reporter answered.

Adam smiled a *real* smile as the reporter turned and headed back across the parking lot, followed by the others.

"Where are you going?" Kyle shouted. He turned to Liz, his eyes practically popping out of his head. "What did you *tell* them?"

"Only the truth," Liz said with a shrug. Then she turned back toward the museum, tugging Adam by the hand. He fell into step with her, grinning like a child.

"You're amazing," he told Liz.

"I know." She grinned back at him. "It's a curse."

Max rubbed the silk of one of Isabel's blouses between his fingers, allowing a cluster of the beings to experience it. So soft. And made by worms. And—

Out of nowhere a tidal wave of fury hit Max. A massive group of beings swept the curious cluster away, and a series of demands were flung out.

Where was the second Stone? Where was the betrayer?

Max sank to his knees, the raw, pulsating anger incapacitating him. All he could do was allow it to wash over him, scalding. So hot, it turned the air to steam that singed Max's lungs.

The Stone! The Stone! The Stone!

The words were like red-hot brands on Max's skin.

You must find it! You must destroy the betrayer!

The wrath brought blisters up on his back, blisters on top of blisters. One of them burst open, and the coolness in that one small patch of skin brought tears of relief to Max's eyes.

You must destroy the betrayer! You must—

"Stop!" Max cried, not knowing whether he was using his voice or simply hurling the thought into the ocean of auras. "Stop! You're going to kill me."

The fury receded, just slightly. Max seized the opportunity and jammed the volume down on the consciousness, using all his will to keep his connection as low as possible.

He lowered his head and remained crouched on the floor of Isabel's room. You're all right, he told himself. He forced himself to study his arms. See? No brands. No burns. You're completely fine.

The sensation had been so powerful that even while staring at his unharmed skin, Max had a hard time accepting that he was even alive after what he'd experienced.

He slowly climbed to his feet. "Why am I in front of Izzy's closet?" he muttered.

Then he remembered. Some of the beings had wanted to experience the texture of silk. They'd have to wait. No way was he going to allow the volume of the consciousness back up.

He turned and headed to the door, then froze. That's not why he'd come in here. He bolted back to the closet. He'd come in here to see if any of Isabel's clothes were missing. He'd been afraid she and Michael had taken off, and he'd wanted to check it out.

Nothing should have been more important than that. And he'd been playing personal shopper to some of the beings. Max started whipping through the hangers in the closet. Why did Isabel have to have so damn many clothes? How was he supposed to know if anything was missing? She'd have to take a three-month supply for him to—

Max looked down at the floor, and his knees turned to oatmeal. She was gone. Her suitcase was gone, so she was gone.

He immediately turned toward Isabel's night table. The communication crystals were still there, right where he'd left them.

His entire body seemed to crumble, and Max lowered himself shakily onto the bed. His sister was gone, and she'd left behind the one thing that could save her.

Max doubled over. "Oh, God, Isabel. What did you do?"

TEN

"Turn it off!" Isabel begged, pointing at the television, where a particularly obnoxious episode of a daytime talk show was playing.

"Jerry's the man," Michael told her from his spot propped up on the motel's other twin bed.

"Turn it off!" Isabel shrieked. The sound of her own voice tore through her head, leaving her gray matter pulsing.

Michael leaped toward the television, but not before the Springer audience went into another round of "Jerry! Jerry! Jerry!" The words ripped into the delicate membranes of her inner ears, the pain so intense, she could feel it through her entire body. "Too loud," she whispered.

A second later Michael had the sound off. But he couldn't turn off the sound of his breathing. The sound of her own breathing. The sound of the hideous curtains brushing against the dirty window. All of these sounds were amplified to the point that Isabel was sure would drive her insane. She squeezed her eyes shut, as if that would somehow make the sounds softer.

A finger tapped her shoulder lightly. She opened her eyes halfway, and Michael held a sheet of the motel's bleached-out stationery in front of her face. He'd written a note in all caps.

HANG ON. ONLY TEN MORE SECS.

He dropped the paper and sat down next to her on her bed. He held out his hands, all ten fingers up.

"One," he mouthed as he folded one of the fingers down.

The rasping sound of the skin of his finger brushing against the skin of his palm made Isabel's teeth feel electrified, but she kept her eyes on Michael's hands as he continued his countdown. When he had three fingers still up, the bout passed.

Isabel wrapped both her hands around one of his. "Thanks," she whispered.

"You want water? More blankets? Anything?" He sounded so eager to do something for her.

"Just sit here with me, okay?" Isabel asked, tightening her grip on his hand.

Michael nodded. He turned his head toward the TV, but not before Isabel caught the sheen of unshed tears coating his eyes.

Poor Michael. Poor her. Poor everybody.

Oh, stop it, she ordered herself. She turned her attention to the TV, too. Poor people on the show was more like it. They all needed someone to dress them in the morning. And the hair—forget about it.

Everyone on the screen should shave their heads and try again.

"See, here's the deal," Michael said in a bad Texan accent, imitating one of Jerry's guests. "My girlfriend, she likes to dress like a man. Which is okay. Except that whenever she does, she keeps telling me that I'm fat, and it really, really hurts my feelings."

"That's way too tame for Jerry," Isabel told him. "It's more like, I can't go to bed with my girlfriend unless I dress like the Easter Bunny and my girlfriend dresses—" She paused and struggled to pull in a breath. "Dresses like a giant polka-dot egg."

Michael laughed. He was obviously relieved to see her talking again. "Why polka dot?" he asked.

"That's . . . that's the only part that . . ." Isabel had to stop for breath again. Suddenly she couldn't breathe and talk at the same time anymore. ". . . sounds strange to you?"

"Well, yeah," Michael said, struggling to keep a straight face. He used the edge of his flannel shirt to wipe the beads of sweat off her upper lip. "You sure you don't want some water?" he asked.

"That . . . sounds good," she answered. She wanted to give him something to do, but she wasn't sure she'd be able to get the water down. Her body was changing—drying up inside. Withering. She could feel it. And she wasn't sure that her esophagus would be able to handle bringing down the water. It might just . . . crumble.

Michael rushed back from the bathroom, holding a plastic cup almost overflowing with water. He sat down next to her again, slowly, careful not to jar her, then cradled her shoulders and brought the glass to her lips. She managed a tiny sip but shook her head when he wanted to give her more.

"Keep . . . holding me," she said. Michael set the glass on the night table and stretched out on his side next to her, arm still around her shoulders. "I think . . ." She drew in a wheezing breath. ". . . you should ask Maria to dress up . . . like an egg for you."

Michael used his sleeve to blot her forehead. "Okay, you're officially delirious," he told her. His voice was casual, but his gray eyes were serious and watchful.

Isabel tried to moisten her lips, but her tongue was too dry. Little pieces of skin were flaking off it. "She . . . loves you."

And Isabel knew Michael would need Maria. Especially if— Isabel let the thought slip away.

Of all the humans, Maria was the one he'd really let in. Isabel suspected that he might have revealed even more to Maria than he had to Isabel and Max. Things about his foster homes. He'd never talked about his foster homes to Isabel, close as they were.

"She loves . . . you," Isabel repeated.

Michael rubbed his spiky black hair with his free hand. "I don't know what I'm supposed to say to that," he muttered. He leaned closer until his face was inches from

118

hers. "Look, Isabel, I don't know how much longer. . . . I think I should teleport and get the crystals. Just in case."

"No!" Isabel cried. Then she started to cough so hard, she feared she'd shake her body apart.

"Maybe there was something Trevor had to do to survive the *akino*. Neither of us thought of that," Michael exploded when her coughing fit had passed. "You can't expect me to let you die."

Isabel reached up and cupped his face with her hands. "You have to. Do you hear me?" she demanded fiercely. She sucked as much breath as she could into her withered lungs. "It's *my* decision."

She looked him in the eye to make sure he absolutely understood her.

"Mine."

"They're gone," Max announced, glancing from Liz to Adam to Maria as soon as they were all seated in Michael and Adam's kitchen. "If they teleported, they could be anywhere."

"Michael's car is gone, too," Adam volunteered. He pulled his chair closer to the kitchen table, moving it closer to Liz's chair at the same time. She was glad he had. Now she could feel the warmth of his body radiating into hers, although their shoulders weren't quite touching.

Max let out a harsh laugh. "Oh, good. Then we should have no problem finding them. There are so few places you can drive."

Liz reached over and touched Adam's arm lightly, trying to signal him that he shouldn't take what Max said personally. She thought she caught a flicker of emotion on Max's face as he noticed the touch, but who knew what had caused it? Maybe the consciousness had expressed a need to know the composition of her nail polish or what the significance of her silver snake bracelet was.

Or maybe, just maybe, in that moment Max had been Max enough to experience a twinge of jealousy. She always used to know what he was thinking, but lately she had no idea. It was as if he existed in two worlds at the same time, and any reaction he had could be to something she couldn't see or hear or really understand.

"Michael won't let anything happen to her," Maria said. She twined one of her curls around her fingers so tightly, Liz expected her to give a yelp of pain. "If she gets too bad, he'll teleport back for the crystals."

"You're forgetting he's as terrified of joining the consciousness as she is," Max said. He tilted back his chair and snagged the plastic bottle of dish-washing soap off the counter. He squirted a little bit onto his finger and rubbed it into his skin. Liz and Maria exchanged a worried glance.

"Could you contact Michael on the dream plane?" Liz asked Max. He raised his finger and sniffed the soap. "Max! I said could you—"

"I heard you," Max answered. "But what would I tell him? He knows what's going to happen. He knows Isabel's going to die." Max jerked to his feet, knocking over the chair. "If that's not enough to convince him, what would?"

"What about Trevor?" Maria asked. She reached down and righted Max's chair. "If we could contact him—"

"Yeah, Maria, let's go find the guy who tried to kill me," Max snapped, his eyes flashing. Liz had never seen him so angry. It was almost comforting to see that he was so emotionally involved in something on this planet.

"We're all just trying to come up with some way—any way—to help Isabel," Liz reminded him firmly.

"I know," Max answered. He sounded so exhausted, so hopeless, that Liz longed to rush over and wrap her arms around him. But that wasn't possible. Not anymore. And anyway, it might end up being the consciousness that felt most of the embrace, and Liz couldn't deal with that.

Max wandered over to the fridge, opened the freezer door, and stuck his head inside.

"What is he doing?" Adam whispered. Liz shrugged, her heart heavy. The consciousness probably wanted to feel winter.

"The only reason I suggested Trevor is that there's at least a chance he was telling the truth about surviving the *akino* without making the connection," Maria continued. Max didn't move or acknowledge her in the slightest. His head was still in the freezer. "If there's even a chance that he could tell us how—"

"Wait a second!" Liz exclaimed, suddenly seeing everything perfectly clearly. "That's where they'd go. To Trevor."

"Michael hates Trevor," Max said, his voice coming out distorted by the freezer.

"I know. But Michael won't let Isabel die. And he won't force her to join the consciousness," Liz answered in a rush. "Trevor is his only alternative."

Max banged his head on the top of the freezer as he turned to face her. "That just leaves us with one little problem—we have no idea how to find Trevor, either," he said. "Adam, do you know if they've been in contact?"

"I don't think so," Adam answered, looking at the floor.

Silence filled the kitchen.

"Where is Alex, anyway?" Maria suddenly demanded.

"Um, I think he's at the movies with some girl," Liz answered, piling her long hair on top of her head and then letting it coil down her back.

Maria stood up and grabbed her coat. "I'll be back," she told them, attempting an Arnold accent. She picked up the keys to Max's Jeep from the table and rushed out of the kitchen.

"Where is she going?" Max asked, sitting down again.

"Don't look at me," Liz replied quietly, acutely aware that she was now alone with Max and Adam.

"So what do we do now?" Adam asked, his gaze flicking from Max to Liz.

"There's nothing we can do," Liz said, hating to admit it. At that moment all she really wanted to do was run after Maria—get the heck out of here ASAP. "We just have to wait and hope Michael decides to contact us."

Adam took her hand and twined her fingers with his. Liz caught another flash of emotion from Max. She automatically started to pull her hand away. Max had enough to deal with right now.

But as she watched, his eyes went dull and lifeless, his mouth slackening. Liz tightened her fingers around Adam's and tried to think only about the feeling of his warm hand.

Maria pulled the Jeep up to the mall entrance closest to the movie theater, tires squealing.

"That's not a parking place," someone shouted. She didn't answer. She ran to the doors and burst into the mall, then raced down the walkway to the movie theater, through those doors, and straight past the usher.

"I didn't see a ticket," he called after her.

"I don't have one," Maria answered, heading toward the closest of the multiplex's screens. The usher snagged her by the elbow.

"You're not going anywhere without a ticket," he said.

Why couldn't it be someone from school? she thought. Why did it have to be some Guffman High guy who acted like having a flashlight was only one step down from a badge and a gun?

"Here's what's going to happen," Maria told him, going into full Arnold mode. "I'm checking each theater until I find my friend, then we are both leaving."

"You are not—," the movie cop began.

"If you don't let go of my arm, I'm going to start screaming about roaches in my popcorn and a rat tail in my Twizzlers and—"

The Guffman kid turned a red that perfectly matched his cheesy uniform vest. "Fine. Okay. You can go in," he said quickly, releasing her elbow. "But don't bother any of the other paying customers."

"Thanks, sweetie," Maria said over her shoulder. She plunged through the closest double doors and waited impatiently for her eyes to adjust. Then she scanned the rows for Alex. The theater was packed. It was going to take way too long.

Maria marched to the front of the theater and positioned herself in front of the screen, ignoring the popcorn, Hot Tamales, and Junior mints that immediately started flying at her. "Alex Manes, if you're in here, you have three seconds to get your butt into the lobby."

She didn't see anyone stand up, so she bolted

back down the aisle, her feet making sucking sounds where someone had spilled a giant soda, and flew back into the lobby. The next auditorium was playing a Julia Roberts flick. Perfect date bait, she thought. This is where he'll be.

This time she didn't bother going to the front of the theater. She just swung open the doors and bellowed, "Alex Manes. I know you're in there. Get your skinny white butt out here—now!"

A tall figure in the back row stood up. "Maria?"

"That's right. I need to talk to you," she yelled.

"Is that your girlfriend or something?" a female voice asked over the shouts of "shut up" from the rest of the audience.

"No, I'm his mother," Maria called back. "And I'm taking him home."

Alex sidestepped out of the row of seats and reached Maria in four long strides. He propelled her back into the lobby and closed the door behind them.

"What is your problem?" he demanded.

"My problem is that just because you happen to have become a babe, you've totally forgotten who your friends really are," Maria snapped.

"And I should do what? Spend every second with the UFO-lovers club?" Alex demanded, crossing his arms over his chest.

"What you should do is stop thinking with whatever it is you've been thinking with and start thinking with your brain." Maria roughly brushed some popcorn crumbs off the front of his sweater. "We need you, Alex."

He pulled two Hot Tamales out of her hair, not bothering to be gentle. "I'm not helping you go after DuPris, if that's what this is about," Alex answered, his voice low. "There is nothing we can do against his power. We—"

"This isn't about DuPris. It's about Isabel," Maria told him.

Some of the color instantly left Alex's face, and Maria knew she had his attention.

"Tell me," he demanded. He pulled her over to one of the padded benches in front of the bathrooms, as far away from the usher as they could get.

"She entered her *akino,* which you'd know if you hadn't decided to become Roswell's own sex bunny," Maria said.

"It's the girls who are the bunnies," Alex corrected, rubbing the back of his neck. "Did Isabel make the connection to the consciousness?"

"No. She refused." Maria felt un-Arnold tears sting her eyes. "Isabel and Michael took off somewhere without the communication crystals. She's out there someplace dying, and we don't know how to find her."

"Oh, my God," Alex said, his face almost completely white. "I still don't know what you want me to do, but I'm there."

Maria gave him a fast hug. "I knew you would be." She checked over her shoulder to make sure the usher wasn't listening. He was twirling his flashlight like a cowboy and replacing it in an imaginary holster. Not a problem.

"When we were trying to get you back from you know where, your father found DuPris before we did," Maria explained. "He must have some kind of Clean Slate tracking device. You've got to get it from him."

Alex nodded. "It's not going to be easy. My dad has refused to answer even one question about his connection to Clean Slate. But I'll get it done."

He stood up and pulled Maria to her feet, and they headed for the exit. "You'll have to drive me."

"Oh, your girls pick *you* up, huh, stud?" Maria teased, relief making her giddy. "Wait a sec," she said as they reached the doors. She hurried over to the concession stand and grabbed a handful of napkins. The usher looked like he wanted to say something but didn't.

Maria rushed back over to Alex and handed him the napkins. He raised an eyebrow at her.

"I know your dad well enough to be sure he's not going to want to listen to you if you have lipstick all over your face," she explained.

ELEVEN

Michael watched Isabel sleep, hoping it was only sleep, hoping she hadn't slipped into unconsciousness. His arm was numb beneath her shoulders, and his right leg was cramping from his awkward position lying on the edge of the twin bed, but he didn't move. He wanted to stay as close to Isabel as he could get. Just listening to her breathe those horrible wheezing breaths. Knowing she was still with him.

She rolled her head toward him, sending pins and needles through his numb arm.

"You awake?" he asked softly.

"Barely," she answered. "I was having this dream . . . where I was being buried . . . in the sand. At first it . . . was fun, but all the little grains kept . . . coming down, and then I could . . . hardly breathe."

"I want to connect with you. I know I can't really heal you, but maybe I can make you feel a little better," Michael told her. He wished he could somehow pull her pain into his own body. It hurt more to see Izzy hurting than it would to actually experience the physical sensations himself.

"Okay," Isabel answered. Michael inched his arm

out from under her, then moved the covers down a little and placed his hands on her chest, just below her throat.

"Your hands are . . . like Trevor's," she murmured. She paused to take a breath. "Or his are . . . like yours. I noticed that . . . when we danced."

Was she totally out of it now? Did she even know what she was saying?

"At the party . . . in the museum," she continued. "I thought . . . maybe Trevor and I . . . he's like you . . . but without the . . . feels-like-my-brother thing."

"Don't waste your breath talking about that," Michael told her. "Don't talk at all right now. Let me make the connection."

All he had to do was think the name Isabel, and a rush of images swept over him. Many of the images were almost as familiar to him as those from his own life because so much of his life had been spent with Isabel.

A glistening ship with shimmering sides that looked almost liquid. Max laughing. A sizzling rainbow of auras in a cave. Michael running his hands through his hair. A burned doll.

And he was in. Connected. His second heartbeat was pounding so quickly, it scared him.

Slowly Michael used his mind to examine her body—their body. The contrast between her internal organs and his own was so huge that Michael almost had to break the connection. If she can feel it, you can look at it, he told himself.

130

The texture of her lungs looked like old paper. As if they might disintegrate into dust at a single touch. He didn't want to risk even brushing them with his mind. A survey of her other organs showed Michael they were all in a similar condition. He carefully allowed the connection to slip, splitting them into separate beings again.

"Couldn't do anything?" Isabel asked.

Michael shook his head. As he looked down at her, he also saw the little girl Isabel, the little girl who'd adored him, who'd been so sure he could do anything.

What a laugh, he thought.

"Not your fault . . . stupid," Isabel said.

She'd always been able to know pretty much what he was thinking. Today he didn't think that was a good thing. What she had to deal with was enough. She didn't need all his fear and garbage dumped on her.

"Think you could . . . find Trevor?" Isabel asked. "Maybe he could help."

"He's with DuPris," Michael reminded her.

"I know," Isabel answered. Her chapped lips began to bleed again. "But I need . . . I need you to . . . find him."

Alex hesitated outside the door to his father's study, his heart fluttering nervously.

"No guts, no glory," he muttered, lifting his hand

and knocking confidently. When his father called, "Come in," Alex straightened his spine and squared his shoulders, shooting for the posture his military-man dad preferred. Well, preferred was an understatement. More like demanded. Then he stepped inside.

"I thought you were at the movies," his father said, glancing up at Alex.

"I was, but something came up," Alex answered. "Something I need to talk to you about."

The Major looked surprised—or what passed for surprised, considering the way he kept his emotions locked down. Alex understood why. He and the old man weren't exactly known for their heart-to-heart talks. They'd basically had one—when Alex made it back from the aliens' home planet. They'd had this short but intense conversation about how Alex's dad had been trying to bring him back. That revelation had totally blown Alex away—and not just because his dad had revealed that he was a Project Clean Slate agent—but because he'd revealed the depth of his love for Alex.

"Go ahead," the Major said. He gestured at the chair in front of his desk. Alex settled in, trying to keep from nervously jerking his leg up and down. This room and this chair gave him a Pavlov's-dog reaction. In the past he'd only been in this location when he'd been getting reamed by his dad for doing something wrong.

"You remember Isabel Evans, right? She came to dinner that one time?" Alex asked, veering away from the most direct route to what he needed to say.

"Charming girl," the Major replied.

Alex couldn't help smiling, remembering how Isabel had impressed the hell out of his father and two of his brothers. They couldn't believe little Alex had hooked up with a girl like her.

"Yeah. Well, when you were, uh, looking for me, I know you found out the, um, truth about her." Alex decided to avoid speaking the *alien* word. Project Clean Slate people probably didn't call them that, anyway. Alex figured they had to have an acronym. The military had an acronym for everything.

"I've told you that everything regarding that subject is classified to the highest level," Alex's father said. He sat up straighter than any human being with a spine made of bone should be able to sit.

"I know. And I respect that," Alex said quickly. "But Isabel—she's going to die if I don't help find her." He met his father's gaze steadily. The Major was almost as big on direct eye contact as he was on good posture. "And to find her, I need the tracking device you used to hunt down DuPris."

"That device does not exist," his father answered.

Alex gripped the arms of his chair with both hands. "It doesn't exist in reality, or it doesn't exist technically—because it's so top secret?"

"There's no difference," the Major replied.

133

"You know what? That's bull," Alex said, his voice calm.

"I won't have you use that kind of language when speaking to me," his father snapped, leaning across his desk to get right in Alex's face.

"I apologize," Alex told him, refusing to back away. "It's just that I know—we both know—that this device that doesn't exist was used, by you, to try to save my life. I doubt that mission was authorized."

For the first time in his life, Alex won a battle of the eyes with his father. The Major looked away first.

"It's the only time I've ever stepped outside the chain of command," he admitted.

"And you did that because—" Alex hesitated. It was one thing to know the reason, another thing to say it. "Because you love me."

Another first. Alex had never directed the *L* word toward his father. The Manes men did not speak that way.

His father gave a brusque nod.

"And I love Isabel," Alex continued. He rushed on before his father could comment. "We're not even a couple anymore. It's not that. The two of us, we've gone through a lot together. More than I can possibly explain. I know her soul." He winced at how gooey that sounded. His father had zero appreciation for goo. "I trust her completely. I know she would do anything to cover my back. You know that, too. You know she risked her life to bring me back to Earth."

134

Alex leaned forward, holding his father's gaze.

"I can't let her die, Dad. She's part of my unit or my squad or whatever I should be calling it." He wished he'd paid a little more attention when his dad and brothers got into one of their military conversations. "I'm responsible for her."

Alex's father didn't answer for a long moment, and Alex wasn't sure if this was a good sign or a bad one. His father was impossible to read.

"Dad, she's really sick," he started again. "She's going through something called the—"

"I don't need to know the details," the Major interrupted. He stood up, pulled a key out of his pocket, and set it precisely in the middle of the desk. "You probably don't know that I have a safe behind the family portrait."

He strode around the desk, clapped Alex on the shoulder, then headed for the door. "Good night, son." Then he glanced back quickly. "Good luck."

Alex waited until he heard the door click closed, then he picked up the key. "Thanks, Dad," he said into the empty room, studying the key. "I'm going to need it."

TWELVE

Relax, damn it. Just relax, Michael ordered himself. He needed to enter the dream plane. It was his only shot of finding Trevor, but he was too tense to concentrate. When he closed his eyes, the sound of Isabel's tortured breathing seemed to get louder until it filled the room. Her breaths were coming farther apart, so there were these heart-stopping moments of silence when Michael kept thinking Isabel had died.

Which was the big reason he couldn't remotely relax. Relax, hell, he could hardly stop himself from shoving his fist through the wall or ripping his hair out in bloody clumps. Isabel was dying. Isabel was dying. Isabel was dying. The thought flashed through his mind again and again, like a blinking neon billboard.

I need Maria. The realization surprised him, sneaking in between two of the Isabel-is-dying thoughts. But it was true. Maria could get him in the right mental state to enter the dream plane. She'd done it before.

Michael shoved his hands behind his head so he wouldn't be tempted to pick up the phone and dial Maria's number. It was too dangerous to call her. He was so close to breaking his promise to Isabel as it was, so close to teleporting to get the crystals and forcing them into her hand.

Yeah, it would be a walking, breathing nightmare to be connected to the consciousness. But at least Isabel would be alive, and as long as she was alive, there was hope, hope that maybe somehow they'd figure out how to break her—and Max—out of the connection.

He turned his head and glanced at Isabel. Her eyes were slitted open, and she was staring back at him. Her lips parted as she strained to say something.

"Tre . . . vor," she gasped.

"I'm going to find him," Michael promised her. He closed his eyes again.

What had Maria done that time he needed to get to the dream plane and couldn't? Michael let his mind go back to that night. First she'd made him smell some flower oil—lavender, he thought. It didn't do a thing except make his nose itch.

But then she'd talked to him. Just talked in a low, soft voice. Something about drawing everything with a purple crayon when she was a little girl.

Michael tried to imagine Maria was sitting next to him right there in the fleabag motel in Hobbs, talking to him. Gradually the sound of Isabel's ragged breathing faded into the background, overpowered by the imaginary Maria voice. A few minutes later Michael slipped into the dream plane.

The dream orbs whirled around him, glimmering with iridescent colors. Michael had never seen Trevor's dream orb. He didn't know what its music sounded like.

"So how am I supposed to find it?" he muttered, frustration slashing through him. The dream orbs started to fade when he distracted himself, and Michael quickly tightened his concentration on them, then began to hum the low note his own dream orb made. Trevor was his brother, however much Michael hated that fact. Maybe his dream orb was similar enough to Michael's that it would respond to the sound.

In the distance Michael saw a metallic gray orb moving toward him. The other orbs spun out of its way as it picked up speed, flying faster and faster. Michael jerked to the left too late—the orb whacked him on the side of the head and knocked him on his butt.

It doubled in size, without any prompting from Michael, and hovered above him, emitting a deep, resonating note of music. Michael had never seen a dream orb behave the way this one just had, and that made him pretty sure he'd found the one he was looking for. It made sense that Trevor's orb would be unlike that of anyone born on Earth.

Michael bent back his legs and kicked the orb with both feet so he could scramble out from under it. Immediately he tried to step through its wall. But it wasn't permeable the way other dream orbs were. Michael took a few steps back and lunged at it, trying to force himself inside. No dice.

Isabel didn't have a lot of time left. Michael had to find a way to break into the orb—now. He circled it, looking for any sign of weakness in its smooth walls. Nothing. He let out his breath with a hiss and circled the orb again.

He noticed it turning an opaque, smoky gray and stopped to figure out what was going on. He could see something moving inside, but he couldn't make out exactly what it was. He gave the wall a poke with one finger. Still as strong as steel.

The orb grew clearer and clearer until its walls were like untinted glass. Trevor stood in the center of the orb and locked eyes with Michael, but he didn't make a move. All he did was raise a curious eyebrow.

Isn't he going to let me in? Michael thought, clenching his hands into fists. It didn't look that way. Trevor just kept staring at him.

Okay, he wants me to beg, I'll beg, Michael thought. He cupped his hands around his mouth.

"I need to talk to you," he shouted. "Please!"

Trevor didn't reply for a long moment, then he reached through the wall of the orb and pulled Michael inside, the wall suddenly as soft as a soap bubble.

"Okay, talk," Trevor ordered.

Michael wasn't crazy about the guy's tone.

Especially since Trevor was the one who'd done all the lying. But he pushed aside his anger. It was not the time.

"It's Isabel," he told his brother. "She's going through her *akino*. She doesn't want to join the consciousness—"

"Don't let anybody force her," Trevor interrupted, his gray eyes darkening.

"I won't. I promised her I wouldn't," Michael answered. "But—" The words were harder to say than he thought they should be.

"But what?" Trevor asked, crossing his arms over his chest.

Michael was sure that Trevor knew what he wanted to ask. Clearly his brother was going to make him actually spit it out. Fine. He could swallow his pride. For Isabel's sake.

"We—I mean *I* . . . I need your help," Michael admitted.

"Do you think we should try to bring Max out of the connection?" Adam asked. He and Liz sat side by side on his living-room floor, leaning against the wall, their fingers still laced together.

Liz shook her head. "Let's leave him in the kitchen. Right now there's nothing for any of us to do but wait."

Adam shifted the tiniest bit so that his shoulder was just touching hers. Liz didn't pull away. But he wasn't sure if that was because she hadn't noticed or because she liked it. Or because she was just tolerating it to be nice to the mole boy.

"Hey, Adam. You know what you were saying the other day—about the consciousness not sounding so bad because you'd never be alone?" Liz asked.

"Uh-huh," he said, savoring the way the heat from her shoulder soaked into his. It felt like Liz's body was about ten degrees warmer than his was, but he knew that couldn't be possible. It was just that everything about Liz affected him in a magnified way. All she had to do was smile at him, and it was like he'd been set free from the compound all over again.

"It made me think about how lonely you must be so much of the time," Liz continued. "When we're all at school, you're cooped up in here all by yourself. I never even thought about what you do all day."

Adam found it hard to sit still when Liz looked at him with full-force intensity, the way she was right now. It's not that he didn't like it. He did. But it made him feel like someone was twanging on his neurons, sending wild impulses everywhere in his body.

"So what *do* you do?" Liz asked, her dark brown eyes intent on his face.

Adam shrugged, increasing the shoulder-to-shoulder contact with Liz.

"I try to learn some stuff," he explained. "I still have some gaps. I read, watch TV, listen to music, surf the net. At lunch I wander around, look in stores. I go to Target a lot."

"Target?" Liz asked, her eyes widening.

"Yeah. Why? Is that bad?" Adam asked, sensing he'd said something wrong.

"Okay. That's it," Liz said, sitting up straight. "Spring break, we all go to New York. We'll drive— see America. And we're going to find you some friends. I mean friends you can hang out with during the day. There must be some people somewhere in this town . . ." Liz paused, brow furrowing, then rushed on. "Then next year you're going to college. We'll fake you some records somehow. Social services doesn't wonder where your family is when you're in college."

"Wow," Adam murmured, overwhelmed by the passion in her voice.

"You don't need the consciousness not to be alone." Red explosions of anger filled Liz's aura. Adam had noticed she got angry every time the consciousness came up. "You won't need to connect," she added.

Adam didn't mention the fact that the only way to avoid connecting to the consciousness seemed to be death, but the yellow bolts in her aura let him know that Liz was probably thinking about the same thing.

"I'd like to go to New York," Adam said, keeping the conversation light. "Especially the Empire State

Building," he added, glancing at her from the corner of his eye.

Liz smiled slightly, a we've-got-a-secret smile, and suddenly Adam wanted to kiss her. He *always* wanted to kiss her, but the intensity of the urge right now was almost molecule melting.

A kiss in the dream plane would have been awesome. Any kind of kiss with Liz would be awesome. But the textures inside a dream orb were just a tiny bit off, somehow a little too perfect. If he kissed Liz now, it would be real.

Adam leaned toward her, and she didn't pull back. His gaze flicked from her lips to her eyes, her lips to her eyes. Her eyes were warm. Her lips parted slightly.

And Adam kissed her softly. Her lips were warm and sweet. She touched the hair at the back of his neck lightly, and his neurons twanged almost hard enough to snap.

Slowly Liz pulled away. She kissed him on the cheek, then released his hand. Adam had had zero experience with girls, but he knew what Liz was telling him before she spoke the words.

"Adam, you're a wonderful guy. And I . . . I like you so much," Liz said. "Just seeing your face makes me feel better, no matter what craziness is going on. But—"

"But you're still in love with Max," Adam said, wanting her speech to end.

"I don't think Max . . ." A net of purple grief wrapped itself around Liz's aura. "Max and I aren't ever going to be together," Liz told him. "But I can't be with anybody else. At least, not—" She shook her head, leaving the rest of her thought unspoken.

"I understand," Adam replied. And he did. Weirdly, one of the things that drew him to Liz was the deep, powerful love she had for Max. To be loved by someone with that capacity for passion and emotion—it had to be the most wonderful thing anyone could possibly imagine.

"That doesn't mean I don't want to be friends," Liz continued, looking him in the eye. "Anytime you feel lonely, anytime you need someone, I'll be here for you." She reached forward and squeezed his hand. "You know that, don't you?"

Before Adam could answer, he heard the apartment's back door fly open.

"We have a way to find Isabel and Michael," Maria cried as she rushed into the living room, Alex right behind her.

"I scored an alien tracking device off my dad," Alex added, green eyes gleaming. "He was actually very cool about it. Although officially he knows nothing."

Adam grinned and scrambled to his feet. Liz followed, wiping her hands on her jeans.

"Maria, do you mind going and, um, waking up our sleeping beauty?" she asked. It was clear she was reluctant to do it herself.

"Sure. Yesterday I mixed up a batch of all the most powerful aromatic oils," Maria answered, pulling a little vial out of her jacket pocket and giving it a quick shake. "It's strong enough to raise the dead."

She slapped her hand over her mouth, shooting a horrified what-did-I-just-say look at Liz.

"Sorry," she said, then bolted for the kitchen.

Alex pulled a thin, square device out of his pocket. "Looks like a PalmPilot, doesn't it?" he asked. "The latest fashion in alien hunting," he added in a mock-announcer voice. "Classic black. And it leaves no unflattering line in the trousers."

He clicked a little button on the side. "Should be easy to use." He stared at the little screen. "Except it's not."

"Can I try?" Adam asked.

"Be my guest." Alex handed over the tracking device with a shrug.

In the Project Clean Slate compound Adam's powers had been tested on everything from starting a blender to defusing a bomb. It hadn't taken him long to learn how to sense the energy pathways in any mechanical or electronic device and figure out exactly how to make it stop or start functioning.

Adam ignored the buttons on the tracker and nudged one of the circuits with his mind. The little screen lit up with a soft green glow. Two black dots blinked in the lower-left corner.

Liz and Alex crowded up to Adam so they could see, too. "I think those two dots are you and Max," Liz said. "Can you make it pull back? You know, extend the range?"

Adam tweaked the tracker until the screen showed the city of Roswell. There were still only the Max and Adam dots on the screen.

"Go wider," Alex urged.

"What've you got?" Max demanded as he and Maria came into the living room.

"So far we've managed to pinpoint the exact location of you and Adam," Alex said sarcastically. "And can I just say, it's good to be back on the team." He reached out and clapped Max on the back. "In case you hadn't noticed, I'd been experiencing some kind of ego malfunction."

"Yeah, who could resist the attentions of someone like Stacey Scheinin?" Liz complained. But she reached over and gave Alex a half hug.

"Four more dots," Adam announced, pulling his eyes away from Liz.

"You must have picked up DuPris and Trevor, too," Max said. "How are we going to figure out which is the right location?"

"Doesn't look like it matters," Alex said, leaning over Adam's shoulder. "All four dots are in the same place—about fifty miles outside of Santa Fe. Which means—"

"They're with DuPris," Adam whispered. His fingers spasmed, and the tracker slipped free. Alex caught it before it hit the ground.

"I can't believe this," Max said, pushing his hands up into his hair. "How could Michael be so stupid?"

"Max, he must have had a reason," Maria said, reaching out and squeezing his shoulder. "Calm down."

"We have to find them," Liz said, pulling her hair back from her face. "If Michael went to DuPris, Isabel must be pretty sick."

Adam saw Max's eyes flash with hurt, but the thought seemed to bring him back to the matter at hand.

"All right. If we're getting that close to DuPris, we're going to need firepower," he said, looking each of them in the eye. "We have to get that Clean Slate weapon from Kyle."

"Yeah, he knows the threat of exposing the truth is over. It was incredibly easy to get rid of the reporters he dragged here," Liz said.

"I guess you guys haven't heard," Alex said, his gaze locked on the tracker. "The girl I was with today, she told me that Kyle is getting shipped to a very nice, very quiet hospital in Albuquerque for a 'Boy, Interrupted' kind of deal. He's not going until tomorrow, but there's no way he's going to be left alone tonight, even for a minute."

So not only were they going to have to face DuPris again. They were going in pretty much unarmed. Their powers were useless against DuPris and the Stones. Adam tried to steel himself, but he couldn't help feeling small and pathetic, as helpless as he had been in the compound.

"Okay, plan B," Max said. "I get the crystals and teleport to give them to Isabel."

"Not by yourself," Liz told him. "You might—"

"Might what?" Max demanded.

"You might, um, stop to smell the roses." Maria started giggling and didn't stop until she pinched her own arm so hard, the skin turned white. "Sorry. Sorry, sorry, sorry," she said.

"I can't believe you guys think I would zone out," Max said harshly. "This is Isabel we're—"

"Max," Liz said firmly. "Wake up already. You can't always control it."

"I am so sick—"

"They're right," Adam interrupted. It didn't feel like his place to contradict Max, but he had to. "I'll go."

"We'll all go," Liz said, her dark eyes on Adam. "This isn't something you have to do alone."

THIRTEEN

Trevor knelt next to Isabel and placed his hands on the cement floor beside her. He tapped the molecules with his mind, urging them apart just enough for the floor to turn spongy.

"Better?" he asked.

But he wasn't expecting an answer. Isabel was deep in the *akino*, nearing the moment of crisis.

Michael hovered above them, pacing quickly. "If you're lying to me about her being able to survive—"

Trevor jerked up his head. "If you don't think you can trust me, why did you even come to me for help?" he exploded. Then he saw the fear in his brother's eyes. It spiked through his aura. "She's going to be fine, Michael," he said, his anger instantly gone.

"When I connected with her, I could see her organs, and they were all about to disintegrate," Michael said, his voice rough with emotion. He knelt next to Trevor. "Is that normal?"

"It's normal," Trevor reassured him. He reached out and pushed a strand of sweaty hair off Isabel's face. He didn't think he'd have recognized her as the vibrant, gorgeous girl he'd danced with such a short time ago.

"And her breathing. It's so . . . it's like it's going to stop any second." Michael shoved himself to his feet and started walking again, this time in a tight circle. Every few moments he stopped and looked down at Isabel, his hands curled in fists in front of his mouth.

He was so worried, Trevor could feel it coming off Michael in waves.

"It's normal," Trevor assured him.

Michael stopped pacing and sat down on the other side of Isabel. He took her hand gently.

"Hey, my Izzy lizard," he said quietly. "Hang in there. It's almost over."

It was clear that seeing Isabel in pain was torture for Michael. Trevor would bet anything that Michael would rather be the one going through the *akino* if he could spare Isabel.

Michael had been willing to give him that same loyalty. He'd stood by Trevor one hundred percent. When his friends accused Trevor of coming to Earth to steal the Stone, Michael had backed him without hesitation, even though he'd known Trevor for only a few days. The fact that Trevor was Michael's brother was enough. Or it had been enough until Trevor had completely betrayed his trust. Trevor didn't know if he'd ever be able to make it up to his brother.

A low groan from Isabel pulled him away from his

thoughts. "The amount of pain—that is unusual," Trevor admitted.

"What?" Michael demanded. "Why?" He tightened his grip on Isabel's hand.

Trevor reached over and loosened his fingers a little.

"Oh, very nice," Michael muttered. "She's in agony, and I decide to break a few bones in her hand."

"You didn't break them," Trevor corrected him. He took Isabel's other hand and held it gently, stroking her feverish skin with his thumb.

"So how she's feeling—it's not normal," Michael said. He swallowed hard, as if his throat was too dry to produce saliva. "What does that mean?"

Trevor moved his thumb to Isabel's wrist, checking her pulse. It was weak and erratic. She was very close now. "I think it's just that the human body responds in a different way to—"

"A different way?" Michael interrupted. "So are you telling me she *could* die? Why didn't you *say* that? I trusted you. I didn't even bring the communication crystals."

"You can trust me," Trevor insisted. "She's not going to die." But a tiny seed of doubt had sprouted inside him. Why the hell had he been so completely sure her *akino* would operate the same way his had? The human body was so different. Maybe it wouldn't be able to stand the strain.

Isabel twisted her head from side to side, making horrible mewling sounds. Trevor sprang to his feet.

"Where are you going?" Michael cried.

"I'm going to get one of the Stones from DuPris," he answered. "If she holds one, its power will ease the pain." He turned and sprinted to the center of the hangar. When he touched the solid wall of the ship, a doorway appeared, and Trevor rushed inside.

"Leader!" he called as he ran down the narrow corridor, feet crunching the metal mesh of the floor. "I need you."

DuPris didn't answer, but Trevor could hear him singing to himself. It sounded like he was in the control room.

Trevor took a right and pounded down the corridor, keeping his head down. The ship wasn't designed for beings his size, and he had to constantly remind himself to stay low. One more turn and the corridor widened into the control room. DuPris didn't turn around or even flinch as Trevor ran up behind him.

"Leader, I need to borrow one of the Stones," Trevor blurted out. "Isabel and Michael have arrived, and her human body is not responding well to the *akino*. She's going through all the usual stages, but there's so much pain."

DuPris continued fiddling with the switches in front of him as if Trevor had never spoken. "I told you you could have your little friends over, but they aren't allowed to play with my things," he answered.

"What?" Trevor cried. He grabbed DuPris by the shoulder and spun the leader toward him. "You don't understand—"

Trevor stopped abruptly, realizing what he had just done. He quickly removed his hand from the leader's arm. "Forgive me. I had no right," he said. "I request that I be given permission to use one of the Stones."

DuPris reached into the pocket of his pleated pants and pulled out the fully charged Stone. He turned it back and forth in his fingers.

What is he waiting for? Trevor thought. Why isn't he giving it to me? He knew better than to ask the questions aloud. He'd overstepped once. He would not do it again.

"You request," DuPris repeated. "You *request*. Haven't you realized yet that you are not in the position to request? I am the leader. I command. You obey."

"Of course," Trevor answered desperately. "But—"

And suddenly he was hurtling through the air. He slammed into the wall of the control room, cutting the back of his head on the corner. It took him a moment to realize what had happened, and when he did, his heart started pounding with fear and fury. "You used the Stone on me," he whispered, staring at DuPris.

"At very low power," DuPris agreed cheerfully, eering at Trevor. "I thought you needed a little reminder of exactly how the chain of command works."

Max urged his molecules together faster. Faster, faster, faster. The instant his body had re-formed, he scanned the room, searching for DuPris. Max didn't see him, but he spotted Michael and Trevor in one corner, crouched on either side of Isabel. He sprinted toward them, hearing the others running behind him.

Trevor looked up as the small crowd approached. His eyes went wide with fear or wonder—Max couldn't tell.

"You shouldn't have come here," Trevor said.

"Now, Trevor. Mind your manners," a voice called. Max turned and saw DuPris step into the entryway of the ship. "You should make all your little friends feel welcome."

The beings of the consciousness exploded with fury and fear at the sight of DuPris. Max used all his will to keep the connection low. He needed to stay sharp, stay in control. If he let the consciousness start running the show, it could be deadly for everyone.

"Thank you for letting Michael bring my sister here," Max said, trying to keep his voice even.

He figured if DuPris was going to pretend that everything was fine, he would, too. Not that he believed DuPris's act for a second. Max knew that DuPris was like a cat—he liked to play with his victims a little while before he killed them. Which was more than fine with Max. It would give him some time, hopefully enough time to get Isabel safely through her *akino* and get them all out of there.

Max strode over to Trevor and roughly pushed him aside, then took his place kneeling next to Isabel.

"What the hell were you thinking, Michael?" he said, eyeing his friend. "Can't you see she's almost dead?"

He pulled the communication crystals out of his pocket and placed them in Isabel's fingers.

"Make the connection, Izzy," he urged.

"You've got to do it, Isabel," he heard Maria call from behind him. "We love you. It's the only way you can stay with us."

Michael grabbed for the crystals, but Max was too quick. He locked his hand around Michael's wrist, stopping him.

"You're wrong, Max." Trevor circled around Isabel and crouched next to Michael. "She's almost reached her crisis. In just a few moments she'll make the turn. She's going to be fine."

"You don't know that," Alex said, joining the little circle.

"You've given us no reason to trust you," Max said, daring Trevor to contradict him. He shot a glance at the ship. DuPris was still in the doorway, an amused smile on his lips.

Liz knelt next to Isabel and touched her forehead gently. "Isabel, please, make the connection," she urged.

"Don't do it, Izzy," Michael countered. "Stay strong."

Isabel opened her eyes. She slowly turned her head until she was looking right at Max. She opened her lips, and a croaking sound came out. Max's heart practically broke wide open.

"I can't understand you," Max said in a near whimper. Looking at his sister's ravaged face was almost unbearable, but Max would not turn his gaze away. He leaned closer. "Tell me, Isabel."

"No!" she screeched, piercing Max's eardrum as her voice cracked. She flung the crystals across the room with a strength he never would have believed she had. Her breath came in tortured gasps, but she managed to speak again. "No, Max."

At that moment Max's body was sliced with pain. He let out a howl as it ripped and seared through his body. He could feel his blood vessels bursting, pumping blood into his body cavity. A horrible, wet, swishing sound filled his ears, and he could feel liquid draining through his ear canal.

"What's happening?" Liz yelled. Max turned toward her, but all he could see was a dim shape. Blood from the veins in his eyes clouded his vision.

Images from the consciousness filled his brain. First an image of himself in agony. Then an image of Isabel holding the crystals, making the connection.

Then an image of himself smiling, clearly no longer in pain.

As soon as the message ended, Max could feel his veins close back up. He rubbed his eyes with his sleeve, and his vision cleared a little.

"Max, you've got to tell us what's happening," Alex demanded, grasping his shoulder.

"The consciousness—," Max spat, tasting blood in his mouth. "The consciousness wants Isabel to make the connection. If she doesn't—"

Max felt dozens of holes open up in his stomach. Hot acid rushed out. He fell onto his side and curled his knees to his chest as if that could somehow protect him from the pain.

"I'll try to heal him," Adam told Liz, rushing over to Max's side.

"I wouldn't do that," DuPris advised calmly over Max's wails of agony. "If you connect to him, the consciousness will be able to use you for motivation, too." He slowly walked toward them, the usual smug smile on his lips.

"Adam, wait," Liz instructed, holding out a hand. "Motivation? What are you talking about? Do you know what's going on here?" she demanded.

DuPris turned his gaze on her, his cold green eyes sending a shiver down her spine. Liz forced herself to keep looking at him. She knew DuPris enjoyed getting a reaction, and she was determined not to give him one. Alex, Adam, and Maria moved into a tight knot around her, joining Liz in the face-off.

"Isn't it clear?" DuPris said. "Your friend over there is being tortured by the consciousness."

"But he's *part* of the consciousness," Maria protested.

"Oh, little bunny. So innocent," DuPris said. He reached out and tugged on one of Maria's curls. Maria didn't flinch.

Good for you, Liz thought. She found Maria's hand and gave it a squeeze.

"The consciousness cares nothing for the individuals who form it," DuPris continued with a quick shake of his head. "It benefits the consciousness if Isabel joins it. If it has to torture Max over there to get the result it wants, so be it."

"What are we supposed to do?" Maria cried, looking down at Max, who was choked with pain. Liz felt like she could feel everything he was going through in her own body. She needed to make his pain stop. Now.

"Listen to him," Trevor called from Isabel's side. "The consciousness is evil."

"Let me illustrate," DuPris said. "Say I'm the consciousness, and he is one of the unfortunate ones who have made the connection." DuPris nodded toward Adam. "If his death benefits me, I simply—"

DuPris whipped the Stone out of his pocket and aimed it at Adam, and before Liz could move, before she could scream, a laser of purple-green light speared out of the Stone and into Adam's chest.

160

He crumpled to the floor like a wet rag. Liz felt a cry well up in her throat, but it just stayed there, choking her, bringing tears to her eyes. She dropped down beside Adam and rolled him onto his back. A perfectly round hole went all the way through his body. Through his *heart*.

"You killed him!" Liz screamed. She wrapped Adam tightly in her arms and pulled him to her chest. "Oh, God, you killed him."

DuPris smiled and shrugged nonchalantly. "Just proving my point."

FOURTEEN

Trevor would not let himself look at Adam. If he did, he knew the revulsion, horror, and hatred churning through him would show on his face. And he didn't want DuPris to know what he was feeling.

"You see? The leader is right," he shouted. "The consciousness cares nothing for the individual."

"The leader is right?" Michael repeated, disgust coating his words. There were tears in Michael's eyes as he looked at Adam, but he never left Isabel's side. "I can't believe this is happening," he said.

Trevor leaned across Isabel, bringing his face as close to Michael's as he could. "Listen to me," he whispered. "I'm taking DuPris down. But I need your help."

Michael's face was all skepticism until he looked into Trevor's eyes. He must have read the determination there because seconds later his expression shifted.

"You got it," Michael said.

"Good. Let's start by slamming him with the ship." Trevor grabbed Michael by the wrist. The connection was almost instantaneous—a brother thing.

Trevor kept one eye on DuPris as he and Michael began building a power ball between them. The leader was clearly enjoying the reactions he'd gotten from Liz, Alex, and Maria. He wasn't paying any attention to Trevor and Michael.

But Alex was. He shot a suspicious glance at Trevor. Michael saw the look. He nodded at the ship, then at DuPris.

Alex nodded back. He bent down and urged Liz to her feet, pulling her away from Adam's body, then he wrapped Maria and Liz in a three-way hug, backing them away from DuPris as if they were just in mourning.

"Let's do this thing," Michael whispered, feeling like they'd stored up enough power. Trevor nodded almost imperceptibly. "On three. One. Two. Three."

Trevor and Michael shot the power ball at the ship, picking it up and hurling it across the room. It knocked DuPris to the ground before he realized what was happening.

Instantly DuPris used his power to throw the ship away from him. But in that one instant Trevor and Michael were on him. Michael went for the gut, so Trevor took the head. He made a connection and started feeling around for an artery in DuPris's brain.

He instantly felt a pinching in his own braincase and realized DuPris had already found a grip on him.

Trevor kept one hand on DuPris's forehead, keeping the connection, squeezing, squeezing. Brilliant dots exploded in front of his eyes, but he ignored them. With his free hand he began feeling around for the Stone. It had to have fallen out of DuPris's fingers when the ship hit him. If it hadn't, he and Michael would be corpses by now.

Where is it? Where is it? Trevor raced his fingers across the floor. Nausea swept through him. Another few seconds and the pressure in his brain was going to make him pass out. DuPris, on the other hand, was fine. Trevor didn't know what DuPris had done, but the artery Trevor was squeezing felt like it had somehow been encased in steel.

Trevor heard a thud behind him. He was pretty sure it was the sound of Michael being thrown off DuPris. He was on his own now. Trevor grabbed for a different artery, hoping DuPris hadn't been able to protect them all. But it was steel hard, too.

Patches of blackness narrowed Trevor's vision. He turned his power on his own brain, trying to heal the damage DuPris had done while still feeling for the Stone. If he didn't get the Stone, he was going to die. They were all going to die.

Then two things happened very quickly. A heavy work boot crunched down on DuPris's throat.

"I like to do things the old-fashioned way," Alex announced.

And then Trevor felt the Stone being pressed into

his palm. "Is this what you're looking for?" Maria's voice asked.

Some of DuPris's attention had to have shifted to repairing the damage in his neck because the pressure in Trevor's brain lessened. Focus, he ordered himself. Focus.

He pressed the Stone down on DuPris's chest and detonated its power.

The world went white and silent.

When Trevor regained consciousness, he was lying on the ground. He shoved himself into a sitting position.

"Where's DuPris?" he demanded groggily. "What happened?"

The realization that Liz, Maria, and Alex were flecked with blood and tissue and pieces of bone hit him. He staggered to his feet. "What *happened*? Are you all right? Did DuPris teleport?"

He took a step forward, and his foot slipped on something squishy. Trevor looked down and saw what appeared to be a section of intestine.

"Um, that would be DuPris," Maria said, her voice flat and emotionless.

"Necessary sacrifice," Trevor muttered. Unlike Adam. Adam, who had posed no threat to DuPris or the rebellion. Adam, who had been killed for . . . for sport.

Trevor raised his eyes and scanned the room. He saw Liz on the floor, cradling Adam in her arms again, her long, dark hair forming a veil over both their faces.

"Should I give the Stone to Isabel?" Alex asked, wiping his face with the back of his hand.

Trevor quickly glanced at her. She was lying next to Max, their expressions nearly identical masks of agony. Michael lay in a heap a few feet away from them.

Fear crawled up Trevor's spine. "Michael?"

"I'm fine," Michael answered with a cough. He pushed himself shakily to his feet. "Just got the wind knocked out of me for a minute."

"Thanks for backing me up," Trevor said, warm with relief. At least he hadn't lost his brother. That was something. He hurried over to Isabel, dropped to his knees, and placed the blood-spattered Stone of Midnight into her hand.

"Work," Trevor said. "Please, please work."

Michael stared down at Isabel. It was like watching one of those time-lapse photography videos—the ones that speed up time to show a seed going to full blossom in seconds.

Isabel's cracked lips smoothed out. Color flooded back into her face. Her breathing became steady and even again. Then she opened her eyes, her beautiful blue eyes, and she smiled at him.

"You made it," he said.

"Did you ever doubt it?" Isabel answered, the old 'tude already back in her voice.

Maria and Alex knelt next to Isabel and grabbed her in a group hug.

"Nice to have you back," Maria said.

"Very nice," Alex added, kissing Isabel's forehead.

"Where's Max?" Isabel asked, glancing around.

Everyone's eyes darted over to the body on the floor. He wasn't moving.

"Oh, my God, Max," Isabel said, tears in her voice. She tried to get up, but Michael reached out and held her back. He didn't want her to risk moving too fast.

"Is there anything you can do for him?" Michael asked Trevor.

But Max answered before Trevor could. "I'm okay."

Isabel started to cry with relief as Max pulled in a deep breath, his eyes going to Isabel, then moving from person to person. Making sure *we're* all fine, Michael thought. Leave it to Max to think of everyone else before himself.

"Does Adam need healing?" Max asked as he slowly climbed to his feet.

"He's dead, Max," Michael answered, his heart feeling heavier by the second. "DuPris killed him."

Even though he'd spoken the words, he couldn't quite believe them himself. He couldn't believe he and Adam were never going to make toast together again. Or watch late night cable. He couldn't believe Adam was never going to ask him another doofy question about kissing.

Tears stung Michael's eyes, and he felt one slither

down his face. He didn't wipe it away. Adam deserved it.

Max scrubbed his face with his hands. "And DuPris?" he asked.

"You're soaking in it," Alex answered. He gestured at the floor, and Max's face went pale. His only response was a brief nod.

"Do you know what this means?" Maria asked, a tiny quiver in her voice. "We have no enemy. Valenti's dead. DuPris is dead. It's over."

"There's still the consciousness," Michael said, his eyes on Max. Did Max finally get it? Did he understand that Trevor was right?

Everyone's eyes were on Max, and he looked at each one of them in turn. Finally, slowly, he focused on his sister.

"Isabel got through her *akino*," he said blankly. "You guys were right all along. You don't die if you don't join." He rubbed his hand over his eyes. "Everything I believed about the consciousness is a lie, and I almost forced Isabel to connect to it."

Michael noticed that Max didn't say anything about the way the consciousness had tortured him. Typical Saint Max. What mattered to him was what happened to other people.

"I want to help you shatter it," Michael told his brother. A few spikes of joy appeared in Trevor's chaotic aura as his eyes met Michael's.

"Me too," Maria and Alex said together.

"I'm definitely in," Isabel announced, propping herself on her elbows.

Michael glanced at Liz, but he didn't think she was capable of speech. Or even of hearing. She was still holding Adam, her face buried against his neck.

"Max?" Michael asked.

"Of course I'm in. You don't put my sister through that and get away with it." He looked at Trevor, his eyes clear and determined. "Just tell me what you need me to—"

His mouth went slack. His eyes went blank. Then his knees bent, and he slowly dropped to the floor. Michael managed to get behind him and catch him by the shoulders before his head hit the cement.

"Max!" Michael cried. *"Max!"*

There was no response.

Michael slapped Max's cheeks—hard.

No response.

"I've seen this a few times before," Trevor said. "He's been completely absorbed by the consciousness. He's not going to be able to—"

Max tilted back his head and stared up at Michael. There was awareness in his bright blue eyes again. "Help . . . me," he managed to say. "Tra . . . apped."

ROSWELL
HIGH

SOME SECRETS ARE TOO DANGEROUS TO KNOW...

Don't miss Roswell High #10

Salvation

Max is out of control. He's lying to his friends, ignoring his family, and has even turned on Liz. Has Max completely lost his mind . . . or is Max not really Max at all?

Liz hasn't felt connected to Max in a long time – not the way she used to be. She knows he isn't the guy he fell in love with. There's something else controlling him. Something sinister. Can Liz help Max break free frefore he's lost forever?

F E A R L E S S

. . . a girl born without the fear ge...

Seventeen-year-old Gaia Moore is not your typic...
high school senior. She is a black belt in karate, wa...
doing advanced maths in junior school and, oh ye...
she absolutely Does Not Care. About anything. He...
mother is dead and her father, a covert anti-terrori...
agent, abandoned her years ago. But before he did...
he taught her self-preservation. Tom Moore knew...
there would be a lot of people after Gaia because ...
who, and what, she is. Gaia is genetically enhance...
not to feel fear and her life has suddenly becom...
dangerous. Her world is about to explode with te...
rorists, government spies and psychos bent on takin...
her apart. But Gaia does not care. She is Fearless.